THE TRUMPET SHALL SOUND

The Trumpet Shall Sound

H. M. TOMLINSON

Random House

NEW YORK

First Printing

© Copyright, 1957, by H. M. Tomlinson

Library of Congress Catalog Card Number: 57–6459

Manufactured in the United States of America

THE TRUMPET SHALL SOUND

ONE

It was a night of early summer, and in one of the years of war when the Islanders, after a fine night, were grateful for daylight again, and now and then were rather surprised to find they were there to see it. It was a night of one of the years after 1939, when all our sea beacons, all the lights betraying home, were extinguished.

Not a lamp to guide seafarers was burning. From the capes, shoals and fog banks of the Channel to the last windy ness of the Shetland Isles, our shores were blind. It was as though the end had come to us at long last, and sea traffickers had ceased to depart from our ports on their occasions, outward bound, and were seeking landfalls here no more. And everywhere inland not a house showed a lighted window of welcome. The final night could have fallen, and nothing of worth was below for daylight to make plain again, nothing of the age-long and confiding. All was dark: coasts, ports and havens, hills and valleys, railways, high roads and the streets of the cities. Our country, after nightfall, was as amorphous as when it was without a name in an early age of the earth, and man not yet come.

In that year, on the slope of an upland of Surrey, portioned small since early Victorian days into villas and gardens for Londoners, and in a moonless midnight, a wayfarer could not tell whether he was in a suburban street, or fumbling through primordial woods. He felt his way amid congested shadows, and hoped he was not lost. It was unlikely that he would meet anyone to tell him. The name of the place, Bewley Hill, had been expunged from even its railway station; the suburb preferred to be nameless. It was nowhere. With the rest of the homeland, it awaited the coming of armed invaders, who could drop from the sky. To give the enemy as much trouble as possible, Bewley Hill had merged into a common anonymity.

The sky, that night, was overcast. The air was warm and still, and our wayfarer could not have made out in the obscurity a shape he knew and could trust. By the look of it, the people had departed. No help was there from as much as a home's accidental gleam. A postal pillar box on the sharp rise of the hill loomed over him, suddenly and hugely, as an affronting specter. Privet hedges and shrubberies were the shapeless uprising of a basal dark, a thickening of night's barriers, from which spires and domes of trees were barely discernible against the faint pallor of a low vault of cloud.

The sight and hearing of a Londoner of old habits, who accepts circumstance without looking at it twice, were not adapted to this aspect of an old civility. This view of a familiar suburb was as still and soundless as the misshapen prospect of a sea floor. The darkness was alien. It opposed the mind and heart as if night had returned to original and unbounded nothing; as if it had gone back to its first state as chaos, which now would be also its last. A traveler, back again in his own place, seeking for what used to be there, could believe that the creative word, giving light, shape, and promise, would never come again to renew what man had ruined and abandoned. On such a night, with the sky brooding as an unmeasured spread of war's somber wings over the frustration of good, it was possible for even a sanguine man to sigh with the doubt that his fellows had broken faith with virtue, and must suffer the penalty of failure with their earth.

Still groping his way along, and still unsure, he felt exiled from the charitable things that once gave countenance and confidence to life. All that had been friendly in nature had turned against him. Evil presided, and was dominant. The sky itself withheld its immemorial guidance. No stars. Weary of this opposition to fair intent, and pausing on that suburban slope in a last attempt at remembrance of things accepted, peering about for but one supporting commonplace of other years, there ahead of him on the overhead pallor loomed the dim arc of the ridge of Bewley Hill, if as ill defined as an exhalation from the mass of precipitated night. Above it, while still he was guessing at what was there, through a rift in the sky, one bright star peered through. It pulsed for a moment with a warm reddish glint, and then vanished, as if it had not meant to be seen. That was Arcturus, so there was south, or thereabouts. Confirmation had been shown of abiding law, and, if it was brief and of chance, yet the fear that chaos had returned, the penalty for man's unlawfulness in the use of his only planet, was but a sad wayfarer's secret thought.

TWO

Standing by the pillar box on the slope were two men, their figures merely increasing an ambiguous blur on the upward path. They were wardens, keeping watch for their sleeping neighbors against the surprises of the enemy. They were alert in particular for any vagrant gleam aloft, should that disfigure the heavens. The foe could appear unannounced in a manner he had not yet divulged. The two men saw the star.

"See that? What's that?"

"Don't know. Perhaps nothing. Was it a star?"

"Bright star, that. Funny color for a star."

"I don't know the stars."

Neither watcher was acquainted with the supernal lights, as townsmen have no use for them. Together they regarded the sky where the most lustrous point of Boötes had appeared, and with concern, for they had experienced the unpleasant phenomena that could follow immediately on strange heavenly portents. They waited.

"It's had fifteen seconds to get here."

"Well, it isn't here."

They continued, nevertheless, to eye suspiciously the ridge of their hill. The enemy was a clever gambler with death, and this perhaps was the opening move of a new game he was to play. He had deceived them before, and more than once.

Satisfied at last, one warden turned away, yawned, and sighed. "I don't like a night as quiet as this. It isn't right. Something is in the wind. What is it? What comes next?"

"I'd give a bit to know. But who knows what's what, except that we're still here, so far? All the same, I'm never sorry for a quiet night."

"No, but it's funny to fancy a quiet night has something rotten at the back of it. That's a queer go, isn't it? I know what it is. It worries the innards, being kept on our toes too long expecting nothing is going to be something. A night comes when you turn away, because you think it's nothing, and hell's lid blows off."

"What would you expect? We're not kept out of bed these nights looking for nest eggs."

"No, nothing like it. But there's been nearly five years of these nights. Five years! That's a fair slice of life. What it comes to is that my belly turns to jelly now if I hear a slam. The missus dropped a saucepan lid on the floor behind me yesterday, and I'd have yelled, only I keep screwed down."

"It's how we have to live. But that's a silly way to go about it, keeping screwed down. Ease it a notch or two.

7

We can't help ourselves. There's nothing we can do, except this, one night after another. Perhaps we've not much longer to wait. Hang on, and don't think about it. Thinking's no good. If the bump that comes is our bump, we can't dodge it, and then we're out, and that's the lot."

"Bumped off? I don't mean that. If we go . . . well, that's no news for the papers, if it's only us that's bumped. If we go, we've gone. I haven't given that a look since the first month of it. After what's happened, after all we've seen some nights, this tin hat I wear does me as much good as a false nose. But I wear it. Everybody's doing it. What gets me down—I don't know— this is the life of an idiot—it's all this senseless bloody mess of a . . . of a . . . and no end to it."

"Of course. But where's the spanner for it? So why bother? We've seen London burning. It wasn't too good here, either. I was petrified that night. It looked like the finish. But here we are. What's more, before it's over, the Jerries will be sorrier than we ever were. It's coming to them, and I should say it's about due to break wide open."

"I've heard that before. There's always somebody whispering behind his hand that the second front is just round the corner."

"That second front! Don't be one of the parrots. I'm sick of hearing of that front. Some people talk as if they lived up a Moscow back alley with only one shirt to wear. They can't take it off. This is the front—front number one. Don't let us forget the fact any more. We're standing on the old original front. It stood up to it when Hitler and Stalin were pals. The front runs from this pillar box to New Zealand, and always did. If it hadn't stuck tight, then the Russians wouldn't be marching west as boldly as they are, and good luck to them. They'd be legging it the other way, deeper and deeper into Siberia. Keep that in mind, as there's going to be no more ham and eggs for us. It's all the comfort we'll ever get."

His companion laughed. He looked slowly round into the dark, as into a future where the thought that, once upon a time, their people stood fast, when Europe fell, would be the only comfort. "Hullo! I see a spot of light over there."

"So did I, a minute ago, and I know where it is. That's from White Stacks."

"It is. That's all wrong for Sir Anthony Gale's house, of all places. It must be from a gable window. Nothing much to fuss about, though I'll have to warn her Ladyship. Her son's room, most likely, young Stephen's."

"It would be his. What's the matter with him? Is he quite all there? He's nothing like his dad."

"Not a bit like, but I prefer the lad to the dad."

"Then why isn't he in uniform, instead of in bed—reading in comfort, while we're doing this? He goes about as if he were moonstruck. You can't see young Gale steering a tank."

"I don't know how he'd steer a tank, and I don't know how I'd steer it, but I saw him busy the night the block of flats came down in the High Street. He pitched into it—might have been a scrum—or else he'd left his nerves at home. When more stuff burst about, the best I could do was not to hop it, and I remember why. My legs were fast to the road."

THREE

In that attic bedroom, marked with disapproval by the wardens, young Stephen Gale came out of his book. He left the tranced radiance of the other world in its pages, and returned to night in this one. He rested his book on his bed, and listened, back again among things as they are, for any sign of their drift and tenor. What were they up to now?

Not a sound. Not a whisper on earth. Nothing. Perhaps peace had come silently while he was reading. Had he been reading as long as all that? Was he the sole survivor, most unjustly, of a just war?

An odd sort of night, this. Not a murmur outside, so far, let alone the horrible banshee siren wailing for those about to die. It was quiet enough to hear the jerky flight of that geometer moth, the only movement in sleeping existence—no, it had settled, it was a chrysolite brooch ornamenting, of all things, a funereal blackout curtain.

How the dead black set it off! And how good, he

thought, admiring it, how lovely, a trifle of earth can be! Yet quite useless. No good at all. As useless as poetry. As inapplicable to things as they are as this book.

What time was it? He was too indolent to look at his watch. No doubt time was running on as ever. It was either very late or very early, no matter which. His watch was wrong, in one way, whatever it said. With a war on, there is no time; there is only dreary patience between one foul crisis and the next. This gift of quiet could change any minute into a premature last trump. He touched his book, as if showing affinity with it, a bond with another existence, one on which he could rely.

What miraculous fellows, he thought, these poets are! They could transmute putty as thick as his own head, and make it light, clear, and buoyant. They could put wings to him, and he was changed. He was up and away. What a journey through illimitable moonshine he had been since he got into bed!

> *I give you the end of a golden string;*
> *Only wind it into a ball,*
> *It will lead you in at Heaven's gate,*
> *Built in Jerusalem's wall.*

The best of these rhymers knew of another sphere than this. They were twice-born, and born again apart, overlooking the uproar. They saw our common goings-on in a startling way. You wondered then what the truth in all that's ordinary may turn out to be. Yet, no doubt about it, another sort of a blasted ball, and no winding required, could land you smack outside Jerusalem's wall any night, perhaps tonight, in one bright flash.

How badly messed up you get though, trying to hold on to the end of that golden string, and with a nasty fact like a torpedo hanging about, and a job to be done you ought to be doing! Once you try to solve that ambiguity, then all the sky seems to be listening for you to answer. How important that answer must be!

He didn't know, of course, but suppose the Beatitudes, once they were uttered, became as much an insinuating part of progress as anti-aircraft batteries? What then? It didn't look like it. Not in the least. But was it safe to bet on it? He must ask Canon Temple about it, when next that expert was in to tea, and would try it on, if the talk wasn't all taken up with real rescue work, especially of the giddy nymphs who frequent local camps, and particularly that most attractive American camp. War, he supposed, involves all things, even love, or what you may call it.

Such doubts bedeviled thought into a frightful tangle. Yet all a fellow wanted to do was what was right and proper. And he wasn't doing it, as well as he knew. Here he was, in bed. He ought to be rescuing Rome from the barbarians, or crawling through the Burmese jungle, or sitting on a raft in the Atlantic not expecting to be picked up. Anywhere would do, if only he was in it, with nothing else to think about. Thinking makes matters worse, when you can't see how to make them better. It wasn't his fault that he was born too late for the immediate use of a bayonet, like a man. Besides that, he hadn't asked to be at hand when the dwellings were brought down in the High Street one night, and another wallop sent paving stones flying while he was helping to clear the cripples out of it. That bump put him back, or tonight he would be in it. The sooner he was with the dear old tanks the sooner he would be enjoying life....

Ah! Here they came again. Steve eyed the blackout curtain grimly. Here they came. More of it. A droning hell of a mob, too, straight for Bewley.... No, all right this time. Those bombers were using the comforting organ stop. Our fellows were up. And at what a height they were soaring, celestially serene!

He meditated. That was where he ought to be, up there. He would fly, if they would have him. If they would have him! You must be as sound as a good poet, or a holy crusader, to float high in the ether, and only the stars looking on, bent on sweeping out this infestation of the constellations; these days, those delicate sisters the Pleiades were being raped.

His duty was there, as well as he could see it. This time, no question arose. No worry about it this time, that he knew of. Nobody could say this time that we had asked for it. Nobody asked for it but the Germans. What had happened to the people of Bach and Mozart? Why had they chosen this? Not life, but its pollution?

It was a mystery. A shocking mystery. Surely it was easy to know white from black, when choosing? Quite easy. Life isn't death. It was true, and it was barely credible, and it was horribly dismaying, but there are people who prefer to poison kindly relations, and that makes the mystery worse than ever. You've got to believe hell's agents are about, hornless, and quite personable, who hate good, and go about infecting it, rejoicing in destruction. And how to know them at sight, when they use smooth persuasion and smiling craft while increasing wrong? Anyhow, here everybody was, mucking about earnestly in poisonous filth, and no way out, and only because of a foul choice.

You were only safe with the poets; put your trust in them. They may look vapory to all solid men standing with both feet on hard facts. They did, of course, to Dad, though for his part he couldn't see what advantage there was in any proper fact, unless a near guess could be made at the way it will change things about it once it begins to work; and sometimes that needed the luck of divination, if sound knowledge and strict logic were to be saved from a ghastly howler. Monkeying with what looks simply a fact ascertained, to see how it will work, seems all right, and yet it may open Pandora's box loaded with all the infections and cankers, and the lid can't be shoved back again. You've gone and done it. Then you know too damned much, and you're left wondering what went wrong somewhere. Steve touched his book again, and murmured:

The game-cock clipt and armed for fight,
Doth the rising sun affright.

Yes, but who but a dreamy poet would have known that? Only a poet would understand that any touch of

14

beastliness, any move of treachery, keeps the general unholy mess going a bit longer. And that was why, he guessed, the doings in the world that very night made the soul feel blue. It made one doubt that it is safe to believe in the good; and what could be worse than that? He'd never forget the question in the eyes of the poor old woman, when he lifted her the devil's own night out of the brickbats and crumpled bedsteads and burst water pipes! She couldn't speak. She could only look up. And she might have been asking forgiveness, though she didn't know what she had done. Her white hair was matted with blood. Dear God . . . that would have affrighted the sun, if it had been there! But only a hand torch was there, which gave one look at her, and went out.

He dwelt absently on that memory, while his eyes rested on a water-color sketch, above the fireplace, of his mother. There mother was, when a girl. He didn't know her. She was only his idea of a spring morning, the sun just come into the garden. As far as he was concerned, she was England. He kept that picture where he could see it, breakfast or bedtime, in case he loathed the way of things. It was his pick-me-up. The loveliness of innocence clears the mind of cant. He expected the old lady of the hideous night of the blitz was rather like that picture, once on a time. And to smash her!

There was no more to be said. What a choice was there! To smash her. If that surprising man Hitler wasn't both mad and bad, then there never had been a word worth saying for brains; and that clever chum of his, Goebbels, was evidently as extraneous to joy as a rat of

15

the Black Death, spreading it. What had men and women been busy about everywhere, that this should have happened? It seemed to him that whatever the poets said of that other war, and some of them had the light within that Keats knew—they must have had it— whatever Sassoon and Wilfred Owen and Blunden hymned of the first grand holocaust, this time there was no option. You had to get a gun. He wished he were in it. He would be at ease.

Though that was odd. Bloody war as salvation? The explosions as sanctuary? Then civilization must be a long way up the wrong turning.

What a bloody mess! Still, he'd never be able to rise to a jolly rousing old hymn about butchery. Homer couldn't have touched the sublime over that stinking job with the Augean stables. Yet he did want his father to know that all the sound and fury in the whole damnable uproar couldn't make him softer than he was. For what rot it was, the stuff about courage! You could get enough sound and fury, for a trial run, any busy night in London, to satisfy the brassiest of classical heroes. One of the girls driving an ambulance about the streets of London went through enough of the frightful, and saw enough horrors, to put the wind up Hector; yet she only expected a cup of tea, after she had washed her hands and lit a cigarette.

He wished he had the brains to think it out. Though could brains quite manage it? Were brains enough? Dad's brains furnished direction for a whole Government department, with some left over to tackle Churchill himself when that great man rose to smite inferior gumption on the chin. Even so, a trifle seemed to be lacking in dear energetic old Dad. What was it? He didn't know. Whatever it was, certainly Father had brains and he had not. That had to be admitted. He wasn't clever. He wished he were.

Come to think of it, were poets clever? Would you call Milton clever? And Blake wasn't an up-and-coming lad. Nor was Shakespeare what you would call a superior person; he hadn't an inch of the great swell about him. He met you on the level, scullery maid or prince. That, Steve thought, was the way of all the grandees. They are not lofty. They never condescend. . . .

That must be Dad. He had just come in. And merry, too. Yes, that was his laugh. He was happy tonight. And was that Lucy with him? She was home at last. Good-o!' You'd pity an unlucky enemy when Dad had a private reason for gaiety.

That green-gold moth was still there motionless. It was quite unaffected. It was content in its world apart. Queer! Perfection was present, all serene, beauty itself absolutely, but only in an insect. And was it as near morning as that? And not a bomb this night to smash thought. Now, if he could fix his eyes on that jewel on the blackout, and sink his mind, he might find the real dreamland. Sunrise wasn't far off, not a banshee all night, and laughter downstairs. Surely the dove was on its way? Let's pretend all's well.

FOUR

The wardens were not mistaken about that vagrant glim; it was a fault in White Stacks, Sir Anthony Gale's house. Lucy Gale noticed it as soon as the wardens. She was nearing her home with her father, and thought what a careless young fool Steve was. But she said nothing; for then in weariness, after a trying day at the Ministry of Information, she lost an unseen path and fell over a rockery. It was not at her fall her father laughed as he helped her up, but at the subdued violence of her exclamation. Her expletive charmed him. She was nothing like her mother. She was his own daughter. He guided her into the dark hall.

That house was so deeply set within stratified cedars and densities of old beeches that a tiny ray of light must have had trouble in finding an exit to the common highway. At one time, nothing common was near White Stacks. When young, it overlooked the woods and valleys of aboriginal Surrey, and had no near neighbor; for it was built the year Queen Anne died, and pillar boxes and privet hedges were no nearer to it when it was visited by Dr. Johnson. A railway came at last, and that started an advance of bricks, red tiles, and gossip towards it. The internal combustion engine followed, speeding villas up to its boundary wall, and presently drove flying monsters over it, making insulting noises above its secret garden. Whatever we may think of an aristocratic desire for privacy, the old rose and umber of that wall's brickwork, built by forgotten craftsmen—who must have satisfied themselves when putting it up—was so pleasant to look upon, that undemocratic regret was natural since now it was put out of countenance by the semidetached counterfeit Tudor black and white villas that surrounded it.

Sir Anthony declared that when the war was over he would give the place away as an asylum for orphans. Orphans wouldn't mind so much sociability. As things were, he couldn't get hold of a decent ham, after finding out where hams were hidden, but all the neighborhood could smell the pot boiling; then he was looked at as if he had stolen the Crown regalia. A frightful profusion of democrats was everywhere. Wherever one turned, there they were. Though how the war could be won without them he didn't know. That was the real danger in war; win it or lose it, the wrong sort of people rose to the top. Dictators or blokes, it amounted to the same thing. He himself was an obvious object for scandal, and he couldn't help it; and the presence of numerous peering eyes and poking noses around the walls of his grounds bored him. He must get out of it.

His brother-in-law, Dr. Nicholas Tregarthen, Uncle Nick in the home, said he thought the idea of change was not only sad but unhelpful. Go where? There was no escape. Go where you like, you meet the gape and stare of the vulgar, delighting in guesses at what they didn't understand and never would, especially if suitable for mischief. So never worry where choice food and drink come from, or over what the envious think of it, if your appetite is sound. And there was something else. The democracy was doing well. It was praiseworthy, and it ought to be given items of scandal to play with. It loved scandal, and the smellier the better. It had earned some fun and ought to have it; yet it might be helpful to add a few bloodhounds to the grounds to preserve as much solitude as possible. It was foolish to try to escape from democracy and progress. Uncle Nick pointed out that only death would release us from the nine o'clock news, which was everybody's meat, and was always bad, and never would be better, never fit for a civilized person. We had to suffer the march of intellect, he supposed, till dedicated and well-trained brains had contrived a means to improve humanity out of existence altogether.

Lady Gale said nothing. She rarely ventured a doubt, and never contradicted. She was too kindhearted, or else she was past expecting clamor and confusion to lessen. She may have ceased to care for what was implied in the inexplicable to give more than a patient glance at what was most unwelcome, yet, as well as she knew, was unavoidable. She was grateful, that night, because she had not been hurried along to safety into the deep cellars; mercifully, there had been no unseemly noises. She shrank from emphatic sounds, even from her dear husband's arguments when they were just; but she liked still less the premonitory smell of the cold damp chalk down below. It made her shiver, though she never protested when told to get up at once and hurry downstairs. She went without a murmur, though deliberately, taking with her some charitable sewing always beside her in readiness for bad nights. There was no telling how long she might be buried there, smelling cold earth; and sewing made patience easier.

Uncle Nick could never be persuaded to an effort to preserve his life. He turned to sleep again, unless the crashes were close, when he was forced to listen to the truth. He said he had no hope of escape from his famous namesake, who would know where to find him, when wanted. If he was asleep when carried off, so much the better. Why fuss? All that was going on was quite in order. Apart from the nature of the human beast, this particular hideous din was only what you would expect, if you had ever tried to sit through a Wagner festival; anyhow, if you had listened to it long enough to know how painful it would be for everybody if the German tribes went tranced and exalted; if those people began to march, chanting their heroic fate, out of their ancestral gloom where the Nordic spirit grew up in fir woods, complete with boars, bears, werewolves and Kobolds. Sentimental people thought the Ride of the Valkyries was only gloriously operatic. Now they knew better; and serve 'em right for being taken in by the grandiose. Leave him alone. He was all right.

FIVE

Dr. Tregarthen was all right, for he was alone when, as
augurs of outer darkness, Sir Anthony and his daughter
entered the study.

It was called the study, but more of disputation than
contemplation took place in it. If a visitor before the
war had to wait in it, uneasy in his modesty, aware
of the reputation of the master there, then that apartment with its informality could restore him to himself.
Glancing along its shelves as he waited, he could forget why he was in it. The room was piled to the cornice
with unequal ranks of odd volumes, an accumulation
betraying the predilections of generations of Gales, even
to the bound numbers of the *Sunday at Home* of Lady
Gale's girlhood. To find a book known to be in that library one had to recall when last it was seen, which nobody knew; or the volume had wandered off, for a
change, to rest on an opposite shelf; perhaps it was in
the stables. It would be found, when not wanted, *Huck-
leberry Finn* next to Dean Inge, or the *Saints' Everlasting Rest* interposed between the first and second volumes of Cook's *Voyages*.

The room had a faint and mingled smell of lavender

and old leather. Its bookshelves made a pleasant hunting ground, where surprises lurked, when a visitor was alone in it, and at leisure, on a day of the spacious years of the past when only white clouds could be high in the sky. In the quiet of it, if a shaft of sunlight selected for a visitor's pleasure the carmine of a Bokhara rug by the fireplace, he could fancy that this idle hour foretokened the bounty of a rich future. That fireplace was as expansive as benevolence, and deep and shadowy with marks of the flames of long ago, and of warmth to come. No movement would be in all the room but the slow motes in the sunray that slanted to the bloom of an antique Asian rug.

A massive Jacobean refectory table with bulbous legs was central, curious with signs of the idiosyncrasies of those who strolled in and out: an odd gardening glove, the *Entomological Review,* the spaniel's rubber bone, an intellectual journal still in its wrapper, a porcelain inkstand, its wells dry for years and its tray full of tobacco ash, a Moorish dish containing a huddle of briar pipes, the *British Students' Song Book,* the last issue of the *Daily Worker,* a shriveled orange that was a cushion of pinned cloves, a necromancer's crystal ball on an ebony stand, a tangle of fishing cord, a terebratula and a micraster of the chalk found in her bed of roses by Lady Gale and named by Uncle Nick; and on that night in the time of war, there were also the remains of Dr. Tregarthen's supper pushed back into the jumble of it, where his beer bottle stood monumental.

He looked up from his perusal of a report on the

stone images of Easter Island, and wondered, as he saw his relatives enter, what news of something worse, not reported in the press, and never to be broadcast until its importance had gone from it, they had brought with them from the secret rooms where Fate is decided for the multitude which won't like the look of it when it comes; but he only asked, "Is it raining?"

The household was accustomed to seeing him in an indolent pose, while strangely intent, quite still, on a matter outside life's press and urgency; they had been informed it took his mind off the upward journey of man. If a book was found abandoned in a place where a book is seldom seen, which nobody else could read, or wanted to, it belonged to him, though it could be Stephen's.

"Where is Mother?" asked Lucy.

"In bed, of course, where you should be. You look pale, girl. You can't blame this hour on the Nazis. They haven't been over tonight."

"Go to the devil," said Lucy, and disappeared.

"Our little Communist never asks for sympathy, does she?"

Sir Anthony smiled, though a smile of his could be mistaken for constrained disapproval. He flicked out the match he held over his pipe. "Mother's habit. She will keep awake till we are all indoors. It worries the girl." He considered the extinct match, his colorless face Mongolian in its width between the cheekbones, with creases radiating about his screwed eyes. Fun could come into his eyes when he smiled, but without encouraging in-

24

timacy, for that welcome human aspect of his almost instantly faded, leaving only a facial question. His head, with its crown of abundant grizzled hair, was set firmly on square shoulders, and his legs seemed less than adequate for his body.

"That girl's bright energy burns her up," said her uncle, "and there isn't much to burn. You don't need to hear she loves Jane Austen. I'm fond of Jane, too, though I'd have been nervous while she was in the room. Our Lucy lives on the scraps she picks out of our funny little ways to nourish her critical spirit, for what she eats wouldn't satisfy a fly. She flits about as if she was always after foes and fools."

"She does. They're there, you know. They're the same thing. Her quickness is after them."

"Too much edge to her spirit, I think. Oversharp. That's the worst of brains, when hate grinds on them."

"Hate? It isn't that. You know very well it isn't that."

"I'm sure it isn't. Call it righteous conviction. Righteousness is near enough. You want to help her, and she won't let you do it. These reformers! What misery they make of everything. A few more drives from their hot gospeling, and we shan't have a planet to call our own, let alone peace at home and an easy seat in it."

The exploration of Easter Island was resumed. Sir Anthony appeared to be dozing, though the twitching of his face said that he had called up his own dream and was directing it. Presently he tottered up from his low chair, his large head compelling his slender legs. He began to pace the room, bent a little, his hands behind his back, as if he were overweighted with what he knew and was using his will to keep a balance.

Uncle Nick sighed. They'd brought the distracting war into the house with them, and yet they would not trust him with its more tasty parts. "Anything worse happened to us?" he inquired. "If German parachutists have landed in the Brompton Road, don't tell me till tomorrow morning. They can't be here for some hours yet."

"Lucky you! No call on you to take the war seriously."

"Not seriously? Now, I like that. Not when I know my extinction without so much as a coffin may be tomorrow, and no whisky in the house tonight?"

"Some of us have to think for others."

"I know, but how soon for others? Don't forget you were told years ago what your pals the enemy would do when the tipple they were brewing boiled up and over, and there you are, just coming to the full taste of it. Will Ribbentrop be dining here again tomorrow night?"

Sir Anthony did not say. He was scanning the table for another pipe. Lucy reappeared in the room as a wraith might unexpectedly shape in the air. "Don't listen to him, Father," she murmured.

"Of course he won't. Why listen to common sense ten years too late? So don't kick me now I'm down and out."

Nor did she appear to hear him. Uncle was mischievous, and in such a time as this! He used words as if they were only counters in a game for artful players. Ideas to him were for sport. He turned words into tricks to muddle serious attention. It was wrong. It was trifling with death. She could not suffer crafty humor and smiling irony while men were hesitant over a choice of destiny. Her spirit was in arms, and it was sharp in her gray eyes. She wouldn't allow a minute's hesitation, to give prudence a chance to hit upon a luckier move in an emergency. It was unworthy of a proud and generous soul; and possibly was the mark of a subtle traitor, devising delay. Truth was in jeopardy, and a show of hesitation was cruel, and cruelty is hateful. The nervous little woman, while her uncle watched her, picked up her letters from the table, absently turned them about, examined the back of one envelope, and left the lot unopened, where she had found them.

Sir Anthony, finding that pacing the room gave no ease to whatever was afflicting him, sank back in his chair. He took a document from his pocket, and gave that his steady attention. The turning of its pages, a faint intermittent whispering, was all it communicated to Uncle Nick, whose patience was being tried.

Lucy had crossed to the fireplace, and stood pensive before its empty gloom. She had been upstairs to correct an illegal light, but Stephen's room was in darkness. He was asleep, she supposed, when even Mother was awake, anxious for her household, though pretending to read *Cranford*. Stephen, whose handsome presence and gentle and considerate ways were a boon to them all, reckless young duffer though he was, could sleep, cool as ever, when others were feeling that forgetfulness would never come again to restore them; she herself could get no more sleeping tablets for another week.

She stared into the empty fireplace. Its marble sur-round was the proscenium and its hearth the stage for the tragic procession of her thoughts. Destruction was spreading over the world in a mania of flames. How sleep, when salvation for the poor and humble had not come? Only Russia was bent on rescuing all good peo-ple from the engines of malevolent power. She saw the domes of Moscow before her as her mother saw the spires of the new Jerusalem. This was the day of the crucifixion of the nobody, and what did that matter to cynics, proconsuls, and priests? She stood in abstrac-tion with her vagary, as slight and sharp in profile as an exclamation mark, a challenge not yet sounded.

Uncle Nick furtively eyed them both. To ease the ten-sion he could have sighed, sighed heartily and dramati-cally, to make his discomfort heard; but he only slid his book away on the table with noiseless care.

He had better wait. The printed page means nothing in a room when pent thoughts there may bombinate at any moment. Suppose he broke the silence, with a sigh, or a hearty damn? That would start a dispute, and with a rush, and he would be in it. Bound to be in it, for any-thing is helpful, however idiotic, if it breaks the monot-ony of war. And then? Then he would be trapped in an argument, in a tangle of facts he could not see. He would be persuaded by optimistic promises that would prove later as fertile as the eggs of the dodo. He would be stunned by resounding thumps of iron logic out of evi-dence of no more weight than moonbeams. If the world wasn't mad, then he had never been sane. Would ever a blessed bedtime come again when a man could take his trousers off without doubting that it was worth while putting them on again?

"I think so," muttered Sir Anthony, as though answering this doubt; and then slowly, frowning the while, folded up his sheaf of papers, and put them away, a matter concluded.

His daughter turned quickly. "What do you think? Is it coming at last?"

Sir Anthony's frown had gone. He was smiling, and it was a realistic smile. He appeared that moment to be completely satisfied with things as they were. "Is what coming, my dear?"

"Don't, Father. Please don't. It only means you won't be candid. Is our army about to move at last? Tell us that."

"Now, Lucy," protested her uncle, "give our boys a friendly nod. I thought I'd heard of a few upsets. There has been a casualty or two. . . ."

"Oh, do please keep quiet," ordered Lucy, "till we've heard what everybody wants to know."

"It will be over soon, I think, and I hope," said her father, without his usual emphasis, which was uncanny.

"As soon as that?" asked Dr. Tregarthen. "It shows how wrong I always was when dubious of miracles. But France is the place for miracles, always was, and here's another coming there soon, so you say."

"France, of course, it must be," admitted Sir Anthony. "It's the only shore for it."

"That's right, and with no port for us, not a blessed

harbor, while taking tanks and guns with us. If guns float ashore it will be a miracle."

Dr. Tregarthen got up, and even Lucy could see that, for a change, it was he who was seriously purposeful. It was he who began to pace about, and not the statesman. "The enemy has all the French coast, all of it, and we learned long ago its ports were forts fitted out with the Germans' atrocious gift for the best fire power. It will be murder. What are you getting at?"

"We all know Hitler has every French quay and dock. Let him keep them, if he can. We are going to manage without them. I tell you we are at the beginning of the end. We shall be there presently."

His smile was of mildness and repose at the end of a difficult passage. He waved a hand to dispose of what was but a difficulty to the uninformed.

His two hearers, incredulous, were dumb. An assurance of immediate release from long and inescapable duress leaves prisoners open-mouthed.

"It is coming," Sir Anthony assured them. There was relish in yielding a secret that had been kept too long; the time to redeem old pledges to the faithful was now. "We are on the move tonight."

He amplified this with confidential nods. In full enjoyment of the eminence which special knowledge confers, he turned to his brother-in-law. "We knew—why yes, even we knew—that tanks and guns do not float, and, if they did, the troops would be too tired or dead to use them. But how if we take a British harbor over with us? Suppose we build a port, ship it over, and site it to our own choice? Didn't that idea occur to you?"

Uncle Nick did not say.

"You may as well hear. Soon everybody will know it. When our men disembark they will be sheltered in a harbor not yet on the map. The transports with the heavy stuff will go aground on the beaches just before high water, discharge on the sands, and float off on the next tide. And our harbor will be fortified. The navy's broadsides will be at the back of it."

He waited for this to take effect. "Nicholas, you've had some fun with our ability to surmount the insuperable. Now say what you want to say? What is it?"

Uncle Nick appeared unable to find words for so strange a turn in the war. He stood thinking it over. Sir Anthony heaved himself up, and clapped him on the shoulder. "If you want to see the show in which you had no belief, you could still be in time for the early doors."

"So that's the answer," sighed Uncle Nick. He was serious. "No," he confessed, "I never saw it, and I thought of it quite a lot, though never to a conclusion, for I suppose I hated the look of it. I've never forgotten the Somme."

He turned to his niece. "There we are, Lucy," he said. "Don't you think we ought to make a clean breast of it? Do you know another country, however beloved, that could have invented a way like that round the bounds of reason?"

"We're not there yet," warned Sir Anthony, not quite."

Lucy had covered her face with her hands. She might have been weeping. She had often prayed for this. It had come. It was tonight. She did not speak. The men were on their way to France. They were not there yet, but they would be there by daybreak. The early doors were for them. The early doors. The early doors.

Slowly, with averted face, she walked away, leaving them without a word; but paused, when about to go, as if a new doubt had taken her. Without turning, she called a question to her father, to clarify a duty just remembered.

"That last plane that fell in east London and killed so many was without a pilot, so we have found. It was something new. Is that the secret weapon?"

"One of them," said her father.

SIX

When Steve roused at daylight, it was too soon to make out whether he had come to a new day, or was only stranded flat in the wreckage of yesterday. The room was dim, and so was his vision, with half-lit misgivings. What was about him had the look of being hung with the cobwebs of old stuff abandoned. There was no change. It was yesterday. It was the continuance of what nobody wanted. He would have dozed off again, resigned to things as they were, when a starling shrilled outside, keen as a boatswain's pipe calling to quarters.

He sat up. The call more than woke him. It went to his vitals like a dart. War or no war, the earth was at hand; it was his, and he was ready for it, whatever it was. Here again was a beginning. At first he could see nothing of the new occasion till the prime of day shot across the room, through a defect in the blackout curtain, a luminous javelin. It was as though his private sunray had come in to find him; or else it was the visible penetration, bright and keen, of the silver whistle of the starling. Whichever it was, the black necessity of night and war was pierced. His head went light to the acceptance of life renewed. He had night's dismal blackout at the window on the floor with a wrench.

An arc of the sun stood facing him upon the eastward hill. Steve, at the opened casement, with the residue of the dark in his eyes, was swept and dazzled for a moment in the flood of the uprising; and then morning light fell as still as everlastingness. How mild, Steve wondered, how simple, is the glory of majesty!

A robin somewhere in the lower shadows was whispering confidentially to himself. A blackbird was fluting from the handle of the garden roller, which stood up in the first sweep of day. The late apple tree leaning over the roller had opened right out at last. It was sensational. It met the sun like an answering beacon, steady with earth's own white fire. The careless birds were in the right of it. Steve joined them in his own way, humming

33

the prelude to a Handel aria. The withdrawal of cirrus cloud above the sun on the hill was to show the curtain had gone up.

On what? For the house was rousing. It was not beginning afresh, if you went by the sounds it was making. It was up and coming again, but only in its old duds. There were voices downstairs. Testy voices.

Steve smiled. Heaven and earth were giving the best they had, a promise of good to be going on with, and now we were adding the only thanksgiving we had for a renewed opportunity. It sounded like a squabble. The day was not going to be fresh and fragrant for long. It would be messed up with a spreading infection of yesterday's mischief by the time everybody was hard at it.

As well as he could hear, Dad was putting straight, or was trying to, a matter that had gone awry, and whatever had moved him hadn't a note of a morning song in it. Instead, morning light was due to be thoroughly organized before it had gone too far. The jolly old certainty that he was right, though frustrated by the miserably weak heads about him, was in his voice, which crackled with the tin in it, even if you couldn't hear what he was saying.

Now Nick had something more to say to it, and this time he didn't care who heard it. "How should I know where it is? I've never seen this secret and sacred document you talk about. Must be where you put it for safety. Have you looked in the dustbin?"

And yet the unaffected blackbird was still going it. He had something better than laughter for the way men

34

used the light of existence renewed. No impatience with error was in his voice.

The sun was well clear of the hill. It had caught St. Peter's golden rooster on the spire of the church below, which blazed into view like a sudden meteor above the trees in the valley. Did the old cock come into sight as a reminder that, if you still denied, then you were not only mistaken, but damned?

SEVEN

What was it that brooded over that day's breakfast table? Stephen couldn't make it out. Not a sparkle came. Morning seemed to be only a leftover from last evening. Once he tried to meet Lucy's sad eye, just to let her know that there he was, and the same as ever, but she was adverse. In her avoidance of his signal there was reproach. War had given the twist in her mind another turn, he supposed, and a restless night would have kinked it. By her severe standard he knew he was deficient; just as if his shortcomings by his own standard were not enough to make him look twice at himself! Immersion in war seems to make good heads go sour and hard. Yet she was right, in a way, although he could not screw himself up to her tight conviction of being handmaid to

35

divine truth revealed. He could not. He would, all the same, try once more at the recruiting office, and that very day, and try hard, to do a bit towards it. Dad wanted to slide him into something quick and not too lethal; but no fear. He wasn't going to have that.

And there Dad was, sitting in his place like a disciple of Buddha, eyes lowered, eating without knowing what he was doing, as gravely absent in mind as if conferring there and then with the Absolute, the All-in-One. Mother was not affected. She never was. It never came into her head, to stay there, that battle was on her doorstep, and this could be her last meal. Or else she was above all that could possibly happen. You couldn't tell. How cool she was, in her old-fashioned gray dress! There was not a defect of yesterday in her face. That cairngorm brooch she was wearing dated her with the hour when Maud was invited to come into the garden. She had not seen a black bat since that far-off evening, and never would. She might be a dedicated one surviving from a year nobody remembered, there that morning by favoring chance, and waiting tranquilly, present but apart from what was going on, until she was recalled.

He had but one communication at table to prove that he was seen, and recognized for what he was. Nick caught his eye once, with a slow wink. The strapping new maid from Devon came in, with a sheaf of papers.

She gave them to Dad. The blessed document was found. But she dropped it first, for her big red fist tried to hold a flimsy treasure too delicately.

Her luxurious curves, as she bent to pick it up, then

presented everybody with a substantial fact. They were
faced by the roundest and most basic thing in the house.
She was more elemental and noteworthy than any secret of State. While she was recovering that Whitehall
decree, there at a glance was the robust truth that we
shall never fade away, whatever bloomer politicians may
decide on as best for us. This Nell Tapscott very likely
was not the good-natured simpleton she looked, dismissed by Father as a slut, disliked by Lucy he didn't
know why, and said by Nick to be the archetype of all the
Madonnas, but anyhow a trusty cushion for Mother
against every shock of the week. When she unbent and
turned, her round face flushed through effort and confusion, flicking back a length of black hair that straggled
over one eye, she was as much a first principle triumphant as the immortal Aphrodite rising on a beach of
Cythera out of sea foam. Dad didn't thank her. Nobody
thanked her.

EIGHT

Soon after that he sidled out of it. He strolled through
the garden for the lake at the far end of the grounds, as
far from everybody as he could. Nobody ever went that
way now. He hadn't been there himself since the Ger-

mans invaded Poland, that awful hour one morning when everybody knew they could drop whatever customary thing they were doing, and hadn't picked it up since, and very likely never would again. All relationships changed from that hour. Even today the family at breakfast, its thoughts as solemn as a mule's behind, made the room deadly for any young joke. Only toast was margarined, and nothing said. Had news come in overnight so rotten that nobody had the heart to speak up? He'd be seeing Nick soon, and he'd hear what it was, if it was anything at all. Perhaps it wasn't. Should he seek him now and get it over?

No. A foul repulse in war is sure to find you. You'll get the hellish weight of it in your turn. Besides, the suspicion might be no more than his chronic apprehension. The atmosphere of war, even when all is quiet—and especially then—is a breathing in of fear. It settles in the bowels. Fear that silence is about to burst with a loud bang; fear there is news you haven't heard to turn you pale when you do hear it; fear of deceit in the aspect of the commonplace; fear that what cannot be seen is the infernal next thing in wait. It isn't fear of death—nothing like it—so perhaps there is some good in it. Perhaps it is only one's loathing of pollution, dread of a further spread of the obscene.

How crystal clear and buoyant the morning was! Yet the garden, though right under his nose, was distant in his mind. It stood away from him. It was a vivid memory of what was past, only that, its gaiety the same as ever, for it had never known horror, and never would.

All he could see was the apparition of the original send-off, when the word came, and a garden was the earliest of good things. This morning he was outside it, a perfect stranger to it. He could walk through it, but he couldn't enter it.

A hint of mockery was in its flaunting colors. The perennials stood as still in windless sunshine as if in secret self-communion. Mother's pet array of roses was getting at him. Every bloom there knew he was present, and wouldn't look at him. The many glowing faces were averted, like Lucy's eyes, though here was no reproach, but silent laughter. That hot haze of catmint hanging over a terrace wall was quivering with bees, sounding an energy that began when the earth was first sent spinning. That music made a certainty of it; all this was in a world that had ceased to be his, for some reason. It was getting on with an original business of its own, unconcerned with us and our limitations, outside our notions of what to live and work for.

He idled on towards the shade of the friendly trees; anyhow, he had always looked on them as personal friends, those trees. They were not dumb. They could talk. What they thought of the day of the week could be heard in their voices, though he had always known they only tolerated him.

That beech, the first of them, the leaves of a far weighty branch hanging down to dip just clear of the turf, and its bole a pewter column, used to warn him off, he fancied, when he was very young. It was a giant, and formidable, and stood alone. The ground under it

39

was bare, and within its shade stood the pale body of it, its muscles tensed as it held up its universe. Keep away, it seemed to say. It took him quite a while, one afternoon long ago, to make up his mind to go in and explore its twilight. The dry litter cried an alarm as he tiptoed in, but nothing lurked there but a basement smell he did not know. It was a smell he liked, stronger than the smell of books. A huge serpent of a root coiled about the dead wreckage of summers before he was born, but no tiny face peered over it at him, though he looked round about for it, that day; and even now he half expected an odd little form to be watching him, if only he could turn about quickly enough to catch sight of it.

Under that tree, he had an idea, was the truth hidden in all the old fables about Pan and the earth. Law did exist, from here to the infinite blue beyond our scientific yardstick. The wisdom of the ages, whatever the clever ones might say, was tucked away in those old silly yarns about the silent places where men were absent. And one warning was clear; it came as clear as a red light in the dark, through all those ancient tales. You should never try however clever you are, to diddle the nature of things for your own important advantage, or in the end you will find yourself in a fatal fix, and not know why. Something was wrapped up in the legend of Pan. It was bad manners to laugh at it, and it made no difference that he didn't exist. We had forgotten him, except to grin at superstition. But was it only superstition, no more than that, the notion of the ancients that retribution dogs the proud trumpets and drums? Anyhow, conquest seems to have a nasty catch in it, only noticed when the triumphant banners go up. He had read somewhere, "All things pay retribution for their injustice to one another, according to the ordinance of time."

So it seems. One wrong brings about another as a proper check to the first, and that means no end to the spawning of the ugly. The greater our confidence as knowledge grows, the farther we go from the heart of the matter. It fairly scared him, when he thought about it. Futility was in it. The happy valley the cleverer fellows were making for might turn out to be the valley of dry bones.

He went within a shade of yews. They screened the lake he had not visited since war fell into everybody's thoughts to tangle them. The round of water mirrored the clouds, except where weeds had come through its surface. It looked the settled sort of thing that could last and last, outside weal and woe, and no matter what happened to White Stacks. The wild was already creeping back, the untamed was gathering thickly about the water, and yet it satisfied him. That corner looked all the better for neglect. Some of the growth in its freedom had become extravagant, and a little alarming. It was a noticeable challenge.

He sat on the trunk of a fallen willow. The tree still flourished in decay, prone in the water, its trunk partly submerged. Such an abstraction as peace was visible here. He was looking at it in the sun. It was radiant. This was the very corner to watch for eyes that might be watching him; but no more was there than two dragon-

flies flashing at tangents like turquoise arrows. And there
was a frog right under him. The frog was varnished
and shiny, mounted like a model in gold on an emerald
lily pad close at hand, and that fellow had a veritable
eye fixed on him. It eyed him steadfastly without stirring,
a sentinel on the frontier of the unknown, ready to give
him away if he made a false move.

A voice called out. It was mild but peremptory, and
there was a plop in the water. "Come over here. Don't
brood there in the sun. You'll addle your brains, if you
haven't done it already."

So old Nick was about. Steve's heart lightened.

NINE

"I've had an eye on you," his uncle said. "I didn't know
whether you were going to take the plunge, boots and
all. . . . What? Not at all. Not you. But we have to
be on the lookout. With so many honest convictions
about us on the point of bursting, we can never be sure
what idiocy the next fool will think is the will of God.
Why should a jolly chap like you want to visit this lonely
sump? To admire the frogs?"

Steve smiled. That, he admitted, was what he had
been doing in his particular form of idiocy. He knew

Nick would understand that frogs, as neighbors in a pool, were at times preferable to what one sometimes had to sit next to.

He had been forgetful too long of this seat in a recess of the yews. He had not idled in it since a past summer when he was taken up with the ancient ballads. The adventure of Thomas of Erceldoune was a favorite. He was careful, however, not to mention True Thomas to Nick, and especially not that strange meeting Thomas had with the lady in the grass-green dress, mistaken at first for the Virgin Mary. Nick could be gaily ribald with moonshine and cock-and-bull. He ridiculed the road to Xanadu; he found no sustenance in honey-dew, which was, he said, only the sticky exudation of aphides.

Still, he relished moonshine. You could rouse Nick's interest securely, sure of merriment to come, with any spicy report of aberration you had come across in human faith and conduct. He delighted in the examples of imbecility about him, and could embellish them lovingly. In Nick's light eyes under lowered and shaggy brows, with their unwinking regard, which was cold, there was a hint of the reptilian, but that was lost in his friendly smile. He was a support. He would answer what you did not know was at the back of your head, no matter what you said. It was disconcerting, and it was jolly. He took everything easily, except humbug. What jugglery with the germinal formed him as mother's brother in the line of descent was past speculation, for the only noticeable bond between them was Nick's tolerance of orthodoxy and respectability in mother's presence.

"I shouldn't care to be plastered with duckweed," Dr. Tregarthen mused, eyeing the water. "It would make one's mug worse than ever in death. One ought to keep some respect for one's friends, don't you think?"

"I used to bring a book here," Steve explained, "and this morning I remembered the quiet corner again."

"It was made for a book," said Nick. "I've worn a track round about to it on which you can't be seen from the upper windows. No mental disturbance you don't want breaks out here. It's the only place left I know of isolated from righteous indignation. What brought you along this morning? I don't see your book."

"I came to look for myself."

"You won't find him. Nobody ever has, except in parts, which don't fit. There are only traces of him, some of them not nice, and they don't make sense. Leave him alone, and he'll pull through. We're not winkles, to come out on a pin."

Steve said nothing to that. He hadn't all that interest in himself. That wasn't it. The state of his soul didn't keep him awake at night, or only when it seemed to be at odds with the way the world wagged.

"I was reading Blake last night," he explained.

"Yes? Trying to get away from us? Quite a good method. He was the fellow who saw angels perched in trees. At Peckham Rye, wasn't it?"

"Yes, and you can't say he didn't."

"Of course I can't. What can be seen if you believe it is there is simply amazing. Do you think he would have seen them there last night—or would anybody?"

"I don't know. I think somebody had better see them somewhere, and soon."

"Go on reading Blake then, read all of him, and you'll be seeing seraphs yourself, if not careful."

"Careful? That's the trouble. That's at the bottom of it. Being canny. Not giving yourself to it. No angels for me."

"I hope not. Don't go leaving us and following angels about. Remember we like you as you are."

"But you read poetry? I've seen you at it."

"I should just think I do. I read it for fun, though not as often as I did when in love, and alone in the desert, feeling very blue, and only the moon to look at."

"Yes, but there has been a change in poetry since then. It doesn't save you from the blues. It gives you the blues."

"What would you expect? Some of it makes us out to be unattractively squalid, I've noticed. No more dignity than would grace a good dog. But look round. Aren't we all rather a drab joke? The new verse comes of the spirit of the age we hear so much about, the hag. No sun, always a drizzle, always the gutters running. And gutters are full of interest, too, if you can persuade yourself to get down to drainage."

"I didn't know you had your eye on it. Why did you keep it to yourself?"

"I never like damping conversation. It's bad manners. All I know is that as soon as I hear Euterpe tuning up again I feel shy. She's rigged up out of Oxford Street, and she doesn't look in the best of health. I don't much enjoy the poetic consequences of wet weather on seediness full of complaint. After all, I've known for a long time more of what brings on calentures than is good for me."

"Is that it? But you can't deny the new thing is sometimes very clever and cunning. It has an air of superiority, and it confuses me. I feel out of it."

"Of course you do. What's the good of superiority unless it puts you in your place? Unless you are mystified, how are you to know you are not with God's chosen? A man of your intelligence ought to have seen that poetry must keep to its period, like bombs and guns. Who wants to know where the bee sucks when there's only hellebore and refuse heaps about? Use your common sense. Poetry had to be pushed on a bit by those who could do it."

"Then I'm done."

"Not at all. What a chump you are. Try to forget Shelley. When it's asking a lot of a man in this general mess to tell good from bad, can't you see that nobody will care tuppence for skylarks? They're no novelty anyway. So what about a few vultures? They can't be overlooked. What if they squawk? They're startling fowl, sure to take the eye. Why don't you have a go? Try. It would take you out of yourself."

"And take it out of me. All right. We'll have to let the angels go. They've left not only Peckham but the sky over it. Only the other day one of the clever boys was making a song about morning light, and do you know he called it the urine of the dawn?"

"Did he though! Quite original. Now, do admit his way of seeing sunrise from a Parnassian upland was quite new. Quite a change. It showed his integrity. That was his honest response to his year; and the fact that you bear it in mind shows that he was an adept, for he made you take notice of him. But you needn't go as far as that. I think he overdid it, though I expect I'm getting old-fashioned. You of course would be looking for beaded bubbles winking at the brim, and so would I. That sort of restorative."

"I thought poetry was for that."

"Yes, when we were all bold in youth and health. But it begins to look as if the right thing to do is to add a touch of asafoetida to the sour of existence. Make a song of that. . . . What's the good of doing it? Now, why ask? It isn't good we're looking for. We've got to be reminded that we are all stuck in the everlasting mud and haven't long to live. Come on. Cheer up."

"I say. You don't really think the starry-eyed dreamers are out, do you? Finished absolutely?"

"Fancy putting that to me. I doubt I was ever starry-eyed, even as a toddler. Couldn't have been. Ask your mother. She's sorry for me. But perhaps we're wasting time. It is no good complaining of the way of the wind, or of the way opinions dodge out. Why not make it fun for you? Why don't you laugh at it?"

"I wish I could. I've tried, and I can't. These hymns to creation we get now are such acrid stuff. As wry as crab apples. If that is the fruit of the tree of knowledge, then I don't believe Eve would have fallen for it."

"Not unless she wanted to let Adam down, the old fool. You've forgotten that possibility."

"So I had. I never thought of that. To let him down. To let us down. I wish I knew what was the matter with the world. Life might be losing its go, buoyancy deflated. And there you are, advising me to join in and pipe up about emptiness and nothingness."

"Not at all. I told you there was fun in it. There is plenty of buoyancy left in us. Too much of it, sometimes. Haven't you noticed the way new bunkum draws all eyes—and especially when it knocks things about with louder bangs? That ought to have told you that our sort of life is still only an infant. We're still on the nursery floor. Just measure us, as the noblest work of God, against the welter of archaic rocks, all dead long ago! Then you see what a rosy darling our life is, just arrived. And doesn't it love dummies! Simply loves them. Don't worry because it is always taking to new toys. . . . Now, that's enough of it. Don't go on trying to make me unhappy about first and last things. It's wasting this fine morning in wartime, the best we've had since I don't know when."

"Perhaps it comes about because of the sun. The sun shows things up. The fact is, Nick, I was thinking of it all last night, and I felt I didn't want to let my soul go, though it is only a problematical sort of thing, if the only substitute offered is a subconscious in the belly, or lower down still, no more happy than one of your clinical instances. I couldn't make a song before sunrise out of the stuff in the damp bottom of the dustbin, not if I tried.

I should want more faith for that than I can muster for the resurrection of the dead."

Dr. Tregarthen chuckled. Then he sat up, suddenly alert, his attention fixed instead on the resplendent water before them. "See that?" he cried. "That's a carp. What a fish!" He left his nephew, and went to the old willow and stood there.

Stephen's attention wandered into upper vacancy. The latest outlook on the world, he was thinking, with wisdom to match it, deadens all that is a-blowing and a-growing. It makes even innocence nasty. It blights memory and affection. War and confusion just suit it. And where did the conclusion to it all drop him off, bag and baggage, to go where he chose? Limbo Junction, by all accounts. Change here for all dead ends! That meant he was done. If pity was only in a weak head, and comeliness was an illusion, then he was done.

He wasn't going to try to reconcile opposites. He didn't know how to make sweetness and light out of the slough of despond after dark. It all seemed to come to the lovely conclusion that there was just as much authority for smashing old women, and for cutting the eyes of children with splintered glass, as there was for anything else.

Very well then. If he had to choose, rather than own up and give in he would get into a plane, get off the earth, fly as near as he could to the Milky Way, and drop plumb through, failing to nail one bloody destroyer, one arrogant young swine of the new order in plain sight, and get it in the neck for missing. He'd be damned if he gave in. No world for him where cruelty and lies were as flowers laid in a dusty shrine. A gun, that was what he wanted, a gun . . . all right, but did a gun show his intelligence was coming along? Did it?

Dr. Tregarthen idled back. "I didn't know they ran to that size here. I'll have a go at him. He was as big as a sucking pig."

"What was?"

"Now don't tell me you are still dreaming of angels. Why bother about them today? What a fellow you are, letting your thoughts drift about the empty sky when our army is crossing the water. Do try to see what that means. Our fellows are out after Hitler himself, and I hope they catch him alive, and bring him to me."

"What are you talking about? You don't mean our men are crossing to France at last?"

"Of course I do. Didn't you know?"

Steve jumped up, as if about to run off and join in at once.

"No, he didn't know! What does he know? Now, do sit down. Sit down. Never go out in a hurry to meet you don't know what."

"But I've got to dive into it somewhere. I must."

His uncle pulled out his pipe, polished it on his nose, and then opened his pouch. He went through the ritual of loading and lighting with formal care. After the smoke began to rise, he advised Stephen, who stood over him, to stroll down to the Adam and Eve. "I'd come along with you for a pint, if there were one on tap, and worth drinking, but I don't want to climb back up the hill. Try the pub, as a start. Trot along afterwards to the recruiting sergeant, if his attraction hasn't evaporated. I'd never dissuade another man from a taste of the worst, if he thinks he'd be the better for it. I've had some, and I don't want to be greedy. There's a lot to be learned, not worth having, while wearing army boots."

"Then I'm off."

"That's the way to see it. But I'd pull up first at the Adam and Eve. Sit down there to make quite sure you want to be a perfect knight. Do that before you feel the sag of the cartridge belt—once that's buckled on there's no quick return, except feet first."

No more was said. They both looked out from within the shadow of the yews, watching the aerial ecstasy of turquoise demoiselles over the water, and in the radiance of a space that was apart from the earth they knew.

TEN

The great news had come. Our men were on the move in full force. The astonishing fact swept clean away settled and somber notions all round. Thoughts flew up lightly, and Stephen's with the rest. The show had started. The questioned and misdoubted great event was now.

Steve strolled off for the town to try again at the recruiting station. He had to be quick about it, he was sure, yet at the same time this latest bulletin of war, heralding the beginning of the end, checked his pace. Release was coming. He was both apprehensive and exalted. He paused, apparently in critical scrutiny of the gravel of home's carriage drive.

To think of it! Bursting wide open Hitler's impregnable Atlantic Wall! The guns for it were in France, in action. This very minute the boys were all out, going it. Were they through the breach yet? And he was here, not there.

He was out of it. Was there still time to butt in? He stood at the gate of his home and took out his watch. He eyed it, and put it back without noting the hour. The immensity and terror of the tragedy from which he was absent, regrettably, were all his watch told him. Opening the outer gates of White Stacks, he gazed south from his hilltop into the calm of Surrey beyond. What was going on over there, while good men died, was vital to this plot of grass, this hedge of old yews, to all the favorite books indoors.

He pondered the view, but saw nothing, not even the summer clouds. Destiny was not in sight. He let down the latch of the gates gently, as if not to embarrass with the least noise the majesty of the overture to decisive battle.

Then in sudden resolution he was off downhill sharply for the town. There was need for haste. They were sure to be glad now of any old crock, and if he wasn't far better than that, then no more cakes and ale. An unseen neighbor, trimming his hedge in firm confidence that he would soon have to trim it again, gave him good morning, and Steve started at the voice as if struck. Yet he did notice, as he passed the postal pillar box, that the chemical telltale which topped it, to warn of the presence of poison gas, had only changed its virginity to a dirty green, through years of weather. He smiled. So much for the prophets of evil! That telltale, once ominous of what could happen any night to people in bed, had lapsed into ancient history. Brisk and careless lads over the water had turned it this morning into a museum piece. Unless he was lucky, he would be too late to be with them at the finish.

The recruiting office, where heroes were selected, checked his haste. His aspiration fell faint in a desert area of bare boards and a smell of disinfectant. Soldiers were there, but at deal tables, bent over files of documents. It was as quiet and leisurely as a municipal department for sorting out the unemployed and infirm. Along one wall, under the windows, was a long bench without a back, and from end to end it was filled with other aspirants for battle honors, and they would have prompted Falstaff to one of his jolliest explanations. It had no more suggestion of culminating gunfire than the local Out Patients Department.

A sergeant-major, a pen behind his ear, heard Stephen's urgent request, appraised him up and down with a parade-ground stare, and led him to another room. They both politely ignored a man in the middle of the floor who was taking off his trousers. Somebody there had a churchyard cough, and it might have been theatrical, but it had a subterranean boom. A naked man whose skin had never seen daylight but once was hopping, under advice, on one leg. Others stood about, also naked, and they opened Stephen's eyes to the discrepancies in classical statuary, and satisfied him that the study of human anatomy would not entertain him. He was surprised by what trousers and shirt could conceal.

"You here again?" said a medical officer to him, and looked him over. "Now, don't lie to me. We told you not to show up here till you were sent for."

"That might be too late," said Stephen.

"Don't be a fool," said the surgeon.

He was released, and no bugle sounded for freedom. As a gladiator, he was without the sacrificial meat. There was nowhere to go but home. Home had to be faced. In that moment he saw what a welcome change it would have been to suffer the outburst of a machine gun, with enough luck and cunning, instead of Lucy's sharp eyes and tristful favor. He had no defense against that. Strange, that to a woman as quick and kind as Lucy the thought never occurred to turn round the idol of her latest worship to find inspiring Marx had no back to him. And Dad's rebuking energy would be there, to be met on the morning stairs, firm purpose well directed to a designed end. In some empty hours, too, Uncle Nick could be the worst of it, because he knew. Other people's foibles never irked him; he only studied them for amusement. Nick regarded all human dilemmas as what everybody but a thickhead would expect of imbecility. Steve did not think of his mother, except as a ghostly benison which included him with all, and there was no ease in that, as ease was not what he wanted.

He dawdled homewards to rid himself of unwanted minutes. He looked round for martial uniforms, and, strangely, not a soldier was in the High Street. Destiny had spirited them out of sight. He felt too young, much too tall, upright and conspicuous, on a day when youth was noticeably absent. How to make it reasonably clear you are no good? There is a tide in the affairs of men leading to only heaven knew what, and it had stranded him. Somehow, somewhere, he had missed the celestial tip, and his chance to fulfill had gone by.

Still, nowadays, did a celestial cue ever come, a whisper from the unseen at a man's ear, warning him, Here's your moment? According to the latest authorities it was no more than a tossup. There can never be a communication from universal vacuity. No rendezvous like a Huntlie Brae was to be found in this new age. No Eildon Tree grew now, for a meeting under it with an unknown's dangerous eyes to test the soul of a rhymer. In the years of the modern you never find yourself unexpectedly in conflict with higher powers, and to an end that tries the value of your inside.

The sedate establishment of the Adam and Eve, a hostelry as native and well rooted as a homeland oak of the centuries, steadied him. That pub was there when news came of Trafalgar. The same pond was beside it, with the mallard drake and his two wives afloat and doubled over an inverted sky, and the usual lonely swan conspicuous under the willows, as an old picture showed.

Crisis after crisis had gone over it like the clouds, leaving it as before; yet across the road, where an advertising agent's Tudor villa had recently risen, only a bomb crater disguised in weeds, and one gatepost, marked the site, as a reminder that time did pass, with change in variety. That morning, too, the benches under the lime-tree bower beside the tavern, where gossip was passed round, were unoccupied, except for one dubious tramplike figure that Stephen barely remarked.

ELEVEN

Stephen put his head within the tavern. The bar parlor was empty; not even the despotic landlady was at the beerpulls. The decorative bottles ranged along the glass shelves with the mirror as a background were, as before, prewar dummies, relics of a chromatic enticement that had come down to obsolete labels. Not so much as a match stick disfigured the floor.

He retired meekly to a seat outside. Even the Adam and Eve was inhospitable. That showed how serious things were. The other fellow was still there, bent forward moodily, brown and bristly hands dangling over his knees, considering the boards. He could have been a hatless loafer, except that his crown of hair, if weather-bleached, was superior to a cap. His jacket and trousers had survived all but this year, and might last another month, but that blue jersey up to his stringy throat was decisive, and so was the poise of his body, though in repose.

Steve got his pipe going, one pipe before going home, and then noticed the stranger was shaking an empty matchbox at him. Steve tossed across a box. The man stood to puff, then came over to return it. He took a heavy iron chair with his left hand and whirled it lightly with ease and in accuracy to a place beside Steve, and in it, all in one movement.

"How far's Okeham from here?" he asked.

"Eight miles straight on, and then one more by a signpost you can't miss." (Not every man could use that legerdemain on such a solid subject as that chair.)

"I shall have to heel-and-toe it. My old man lives there."

Then he was an amateur tramp, Steve supposed, but as a prodigal son he was not quite the thing. There was a definition in the curves of his body not to be acquired through aimless drift. His age was not in his leathery face, and his eyes, if casual and dreamy, suddenly turned on Steve under drooping lids in the style Steve had noticed in the sardonic interest of a Cockney.

"The bitch in there," remarked the stranger, jerking a thumb over his shoulder, "wanted to know what I was doing in the war, so I came out, and I want a drink."

"Let's go back," said Stephen.

"It won't work. Not after what I told her she was, and

57

why she was, and looked the very spit of it. She's thrown out of gear."

"But you've a long way to go, and it's a warm day."

"Not so far as I've been, and warmer."

"Come far then?"

The stranger was deaf to this question.

Steve asked no more. "Anyway," added the stranger suddenly, "does it matter what anyone's doing in the perishing war when he can't help himself? What are you doing, except yapping with me?"

"Nothing. They won't have me. They've just told me so again."

Steve turned to the fellow, but the man had resumed his moody contemplation of the boards. A sailor, was he? He didn't look the picture-book sailor, though perhaps sailors never do. After all, there wouldn't be a mark about True Thomas himself to show where he had been, and what he had seen, except when he began to speak, and then only if you tumbled to what Elfland meant. This chap seemed to be one of the incurious sort, too, who wouldn't turn his head to see a circus go by, giraffes and all. But perhaps his tired eyes and lazy voice only meant that he had seen all he wanted, and it wasn't worth talking about.

The man stretched, and looked round, as if he had only just noticed where he was. He nodded across the road to the ruins. "Had some bumps here?"

"Plenty. Too many, some nights."

"Good for you. You know there's dirt about."

"The cats and dogs know as much. Our dog jumps up

at the first howl of the siren. He leads the way to the dugout. That's as much as we know."

The stranger was not listening. He was lightly singing to himself in absence of mind, or lightness of head. Steve also withdrew into the secrecy of his own disappointment, until the humming near him began to shape into the air of—what was it? Yes, "Over the Sea to Skye." That brought him to wary attention again of the stranger, who was like none of the people known to White Stacks. That song was not of London. This chap would put Uncle Nick in a fix, who was always sure he could tell the kind of mud another person was made of by their little unconscious tricks when self-absorbed.

The stranger came out of his reverie. "What's laid up for us," he said, "can't be missed. That dog of yours, he knows something, but it falls short."

"I say, but look here, we know no more than the dog what's laid up."

"Of course we don't, not till we get it. That's what keeps us busy learning more of the knots that won't slip."

"Which only gets us through the day."

"What more do you want?"

Steve laughed. "All right. But I'd give a little to see what's round the corner."

"When I was just big enough," mused the stranger, "to sit on a bollard watching the ships on the river, playing the hop from school, I thought all the best things were somewhere else. So I went."

He dwelt so long upon this apparent error that Steve had to ask, "Was it as easy as that?"

"What's easy? It's easy to ask for it. It's as easy as stepping on a hatch cover which isn't there in the dark. It was a fine night, one night, it was June. That's right, it was the beginning of June, and the river I was looking at, and the lights on it, beginning to light up, was what would make a nipper think he was being told to come on. There was a barque at the buoys, not a big dandy craft, only a useful little 'un, with a riding light. She was a black barque with one bright eye, and it was fixed on me. It was steady on my frivolity, was that eye.

"Then an old woman came along. I thought I was on my lone. She was all black, like the barque, except her face, which made me jump it was so close to my ear hole, and white. I slid off that bollard quick, and stood off. 'Can you row?' she said.

"Now, can a duck swim? So I told her I could and all. 'You're the lucky lad,' she said, 'you're the one I'm looking for, and I've found you waiting for me, so I have. Do you see that ship? She's bound out this night, and I've a packet for her, and she must have it or my name's gone. The boat is tied up below here at our feet, and my old man is dead to the wide, as he often is on a Saturday, just when he's wanted, though tonight's the night. Do you pull me over to that riding light, and mind you the set of the stream. The tide begins to ebb.'

"So I went. Any nipper would. It was a lark, though I don't remember having seen the skiff I was pulling, not before that, and I had an idea I knew all the boats about, and who raised hell if you got into one, which I often did. There the old woman was, sitting on the transom,

60

and looming up in front of me she was a sight taller and blacker than she was on the pier. I wondered who she was, but not much. I knew that stream, and it was only a game to cut over to that riding light. The old woman could have done it herself. In fact she did afterwards, I reckon, going back, though I don't know nothing about that. I wasn't with her then, so I don't know."

The stranger frowned at the boards, as if studying them for the secret of her identity.

"What, you never saw her again?"

"Who? The old party in the black cape? Not me. There she was, but because I went into the fo'castle for a look-see, there she wasn't, nor the boat, when I came out. And here I am in consequence."

"That's a long jump," said Steve.

"It is and all," said the sailor.

TWELVE

There's luck for you, Steve thought. This fellow is pushed off for a run to Prospero's Island while playing on his own doorstep. No waiting. He gets the cue from a figure as plain as one of the Norns, and he's away. That's better than Winchester and Oxford. She touches your shoulder, and you've gone. But I sit here listening to the fairy tale, and then stroll home to read more of them.

"I had quick parts when young," went on the sailor, "and so has an air balloon, blowing this way and that, and then off the map. And what have I learned since, except that's how it was with me? My old dad will say so when he sees me, which he hasn't for years, and surprised he will be and dumb, till he finds the best words in his language. Have you got some baccy?

"Here, you smoke strong stuff for a young 'un! And that's right. No half and half for us. So you see how it fell out. I went into the fo'castle, and the glim of a hurricane lamp was at the heel of the bowsprit. That's all. It was only night in there, except a smell, till a nigger turned up his face by the lamp, and then there were eyes and teeth. He was laughing. 'Lordy, here's the new boy blown along. Come on in. It's bully for you you've got weight. The last poor little bastard could hardly lift his hand to his little nose, and he went overside off Fernando Po, bless his heart. Come and sit here and have some coffee, new boy.'

"I had that coffee, and more. He told me all about it, or I thought he did, and that's how we miss it. It's like us to suppose when we hear the tale we've heard the lot, but the odds are there's more to come, and hell's the difference. What would a nipper make of that fo'castle? There a nigger was, so the ship was going to Africa or the West Indies, where the palms grow, where the things are stuck about that won't let you believe your own eyes at a second look. It was gay stuff that nigger yarned and laughed about, and he had a nigger's laugh, no bones in it. Then a whistle blew outside, and stopped him short. Up he jumped and went. 'Sit there,' he said, 'and I'll be back.' So I sat there with the lamp, and heard shouts I got to know better later on, and the swish of waters, and fell asleep, quite satisfied. There was something in that coffee. That's my belief. It seemed to me that coffee was better than nice."

Steve's eyes, fixed absently over the bent head of the storyteller, saw across the road, in another world, a neighbor passing in his warden's steel helmet. That neighbor stopped to smooth the head of the black and white cat perched as usual on the lonely gatepost, all that was left of a home it would not forsake.

"When I woke," said the sailor, "I was sick. I didn't care if I was on the voyage to Fiddler's Green. But I had to turn-to. I hope I shall never feel as bad as that again, but I have, and I will. I might have died but for that nigger, who laughed all the time out of his deep belly. He was from Nova Scotia, so he said, and they called him Mac.

"Do you know the sea, mister? Not you. Nobody does, for more than a dogwatch. He was a liar, the man that made a song about life on the ocean wave. What's today? Is it? I thought it was Monday. Then I shall be afloat in three days more, which means the moon will be full for me. I didn't know where we were going, that first voyage, and after I could eat again I didn't care, and I didn't ask. I did know something. I knew the name of the ship. She was the *Truelove*. It was on her longboat.

She was a wooden barque with outboard channels, so when she was resurrected from the mud I can't say. She had a ninety-horsepower coffee grinder to help her when the wind dropped, and she was old enough to have met my grandfather.

"She was family-owned, if you know what that means, and her Old Man's name was Burdett, and he was so sure of God's mercy, and that dreams mean more than you'd think, that nobody could talk sense into him. His family ought to have put him away and sold their ship before he sailed, but I'm glad they didn't, or I shouldn't have been there, and later on I wished I wasn't.

"The captain told me I was a child of grace and could come to no harm, not if the sky went up like a roller blind, which was the first I'd heard of it. He was little and old, with gray whiskers fringing a red face, and a square-topped hat, the same as a Methodist pilot, and he went about slow and calm, quite sure nothing could touch him, though touched he was all right enough. The mate, who was a sailor and a hard case, only knew enough of the stars to get them unfixed. He never knew when we were within spitting distance of the reefs, so I heard, and I believed it, for I was told worse things of him than that, and it didn't seem much anyway, with all that water about. We dropped the land and didn't find it again. I didn't know so much waste water was rolling round the world.

"No more land, and it got colder and colder one day after another. We had all the perishing air to ourselves, nothing else in sight, not a bird.

"I was shivering and asked Mac about it, and he grinned and said no cocoa beans this voyage and no Guinea Coast. We were on a voyage looking for castaways. He said the Old Man's brother was long overdue in a sealer, and we were going to pick him up. Our Old Man used to reckon his brother had gone, and had given him up, but one night he had a dream. He dreamt he was looking at a chart. It was a new one to him, and a white cock stood on it pecking at grains. So he put on his spectacles and looked at that chart, just where the bird was pecking, and saw an island was marked. It was called Jan Mayen. Mac said he had seen that chart, and as sure as we lived there the island was, no bigger than a grain of corn, and we were on a northerly course for it, if the captain's figuring was lucky, and it always was.

" 'But you're right,' says Mac, 'cold it is, as cold as the day when we die, and we're not there yet.' There's no money in this voyage, he told me, there's only an offering for sin, because our captain's brother was a wicked old devil, and did only what he shouldn't, but he was precious in the sight of heaven, and they must take him off that island and be damned to him before he died with his heart as hard as it was when he was young and knew all the houses of Tiger Bay it isn't safe to peep in, let alone sleep in.

"I turned out one morning and the rigging and deck were white as Happy Christmas. Ice was bright to the skyline, and the air froze in my nose and made it ache. The ice was in flat fields with creeks and narrows curling through them and no other course for us, and marble bergs stood up topping our trucks, and it didn't say anything. The sun was shining, but no more good than the moon. We lined the bulwarks, everybody present, looking at Jan Mayen. There it was. It was a long way off. It wasn't land to me, that white sugarloaf miles high, its point stuck fast in an iron cloud. It was never meant for seamen, nor anybody else. It stood up miles away over fields of ice where things had come to an end, or had never started, and never would.

"A gale got up that night. It was a howler. You don't know arctic seas, so you keep away, unless you want to find out you don't count. They're not natural to a ship. Her game is up. The bumps and deafening hullabaloo and her plunging about told me in my bunk I was in for my long sleep, and that I'd drop off in another minute, but morning came. We were under bare poles. The only sail set was blown to a rag. She was driving to leeward, and a great swell was running, and so were we, and the floes and a fleet of bergs were keeping us company, all together, close aboard. You'd see to windward something as big as a church on the next rise of the sea about to topple over on the deck, and change its mind at the last minute. My tripes turned pale looking up at it. The gale boomed in the gear, and the exhaust pipe was screaming, and the bergs collided. If the last trump had sounded we shouldn't have heard it. Perhaps it went ten minutes back. I thought it had, but I tried to be like the other chaps, and took it the same as being used to it."

The stranger fell silent again, examining an odd-looking ring on his right little finger. Steve noticed it then, a mounted green scarab.

"There you are," said the man, as though speaking to his mascot, "if you get the fancy that you can bluff what was there before you were, and before Adam, and will be there to meet the next chap and the last when they come along, the odds are you'll find your right reckoning about as much use as a kind letter from Mother. Next day the wind dropped. It fell quiet, and we could breathe again, but we were set fast. We were caught. There was no sea, only hummocks and bergs. Stuff froze in the ship I didn't know could freeze. I froze, and one day Mac saved my dead hands. The coal gave out, and rations came down to dividing up biscuit dust and scrapings, and what we couldn't eat when hearty.

"This here ring was Mac's. He gave it me the day he died. When a man died he was left where he was. Captain Burdett went next, sitting at the messtable, where I used to wait on him, bent over it with his face in his hands, still praying, and as hard and fixed as the table. When the ship was free again, I don't know when, and that Norwegian whaler came alongside, I was one of four left. . . ."

The confessional voice ceased. Steve's gaze was lost in vacancy. Several armored cars thundered along the road, and he roused and looked round.

The stranger had gone. This bemused him, as if he had been reading or dreaming, and had suddenly wakened into a deceptive and derisive world. There was no sign of the man. That he might be the victim of a vagary

67

was suggested in the fact that his Uncle Nick was alone and reposeful on a neighboring bench, and caught his wandering eye.

"He'll be back in a minute," explained Nick. "He hasn't gone far." Dr. Tregarthen rose and came over.

"So I find you here. Changed your mind about the re-cruiting office?"

"I went there first. I did my best and they won't take me. They kicked me out."

"What are our behinds for? Don't look so glum about it."

"Glum? I'd forgotten it. I've been listening to an out-landish tale, and wondering what to make of it."

"What do you want to make of it? Won't it do as it is? I've been eavesdropping, and heard the gist of it. That fellow's face wasn't cast in those lines for nothing. Keep him here while I try to find a bottle or two. I want a closer look at him."

THIRTEEN

The stranger returned, but only to put a foot on his chair to tighten a shoelace. He muttered that he was wasting time. "I must be off," he said to Stephen. "There's nine miles to put behind me."

Dr. Tregarthen rounded the corner at the moment, cuddling bottles and glasses, for he had met no more difficulty than usual with a personable landlady. "What, not away so soon? Don't go yet with this about. This comes first. Far to go?"

"Okeham."

"Is that all? That's not as many miles as you've just covered, I'll be bound. You'll finish the last lap at speed."

The sailor regarded him straightly, without amusement; but Nick was at ease, in the large, slow and confidential way which satisfied dogs, children, and simple minds.

"After all," he pointed out, "you haven't come from Jan Mayen this voyage."

"Our course wasn't far off it."

"What, again? You must love ice bergs. After what you've said of them, give me the hottest place of all."

"Ah!" said the sailor.

"One night of it would have finished me. I couldn't go far on biscuit weevils and snow, with corpses as bedfellows."

The sailor drank. "Nobody likes it, and they needn't ask for it. If they do, it's there. But what beats me is that there's worse things."

"Worse than being hungry till you grow into an icicle?"

"That's right."

"Dear God! Something worse than being trapped on the world's dead top, waiting for the last day! I can't bear to think of anything so horrible, whatever it is."

"Same here. But it turns up, and you run slap into it. Then what?"

"May I never have to hit on the answer to that one."

The sailor himself appeared to have no suitable answer to offer. He only said, reminiscently, "The other chap can be such an ugly swine and don't look it, he don't look it, and you don't know it till he's hooked you by the crutch."

"They considered this. I see," said the doctor. "So that's what's the matter."

Then, while they were still pondering so simple an admission of an enigma as old as Cain and treachery, Dr. Tregarthen remarked, "It looks to me very much as if you rounded North Cape last voyage."

"I did that. Well to the north of it. As far back as January. I've been in dry dock since. Scrap metal in the tubes, besides bats in the belfry."

"All right now?"

"No complaints. Bar perhaps a bat or two. I don't know."

"Fill up again. There's the bottle. You've no more bats than the rest of us. Don't bother about them. We all have a few in the attic. I think you've hit the mark. When the other fellow talks just as we do, like a good fellow, and puts us off our guard, and gives us nice words to dope us before he begins his dirty tricks, we wonder why he was made. Why was it? He's worse than leprosy. There's a cure for that, none for him. He pokes out the fun in eyes, and here we are, groping about in the dark."

The sailor, elbows on knees, frowned at his glass, tilting it about. It seemed to Steve that he was trying to make Nick's words fit his own notion. He then said, "Once I saw a girl in the sea, and she was holding her doll. That's right, clasping her doll. Her frock was floating her, and the sea was all blazing oil from the ship, and I couldn't get near her. Couldn't do it. Nobody could. That wasn't the sea's fault."

Nobody denied it. "I used to say," he continued, "that the Kaiser's war was what we were asking for a long way ahead of schedule. An open boat in the Atlantic and no grub and a nor'wester going it wasn't a pleasure party, and don't I know it, but we've done better since. This dose we've got beats anything the devil could think up."

"It was wasting time," said the doctor, "to invent the devil, wasn't it? We always have our best intentions handy. Quite enough to get along with. We can do things with them no devil would dream of doing without shaming his horns and tail."

"It's a stinker," muttered the stranger. "It beats me."

"No it doesn't," cried Stephen, "the world's all right. You didn't let it down."

His uncle showed his amusement. The sailor turned a droll face on Stephen, who had startled himself with his impulsive exclamation, which escaped before he knew it; and, embarrassed, he stammered an explanation that he had thought the North Pole was high above incendiaries, explosions, and muck.

"North Pole or Cheapside, it's no odds, so don't you

go north to mark the differ. Sometimes we were glad of handy floes when Jerry destroyers were about. Her nose was poked into that lot. We docked among the bergs. Destroyers can't trust their thin skins near bergs. And that ice barrier you hear about is only ginger in the gamble for bombers. All in the game. You dodge torpedoes and bombs on the same helm, and bring it off, sometimes. That and the dark. That and the cold."

"I hope it wasn't on the voyage out they got you."

"It was and all. We had immediate discharge. Don't ask where. I had no bearings. I was only doing what I could to pull through. You miss the count up on the roof, with no day and night, and the stars the next stop. It's all one up there. The dark thins before eight bells, morning. You hope the sun is on his way up to join in, but the fathoms are too deep for him. He sinks without breaking surface. A one-eyed twilight is all you get, and not for long. There you are, hoping that perhaps things may look up again, and you can pull it off, not far to go now, Murmansk soon, and then you're back where you were while you freeze worse. You can see the ship—she's plain, she's caked in ice and she's under way, and the wind draws over her like a draught in a dead house. She was like that when our siren gave the six blasts, lifting me out of my boots. We were for it. I thought I'd heard the drone of planes, but didn't believe my ears. So I dived for the stokehold and a shovel.

"What's that? Can't say. As for me, it's better below with only the furnace doors and the gauges to watch, and warmer. . . . Eh? Nothing in it. Best bend your best to give her full power, and a touch more, hoping she'll stand it. Of course you listen. You've got to listen. The ears stretch out a fair length. That time we got it, and I didn't hear a word of it. I thought the sea floor shot up and buckled our bottom plates. I was having a drink that minute and it ran up my nose. I did notice the bulkheads curling inwards like torn paper. The sea swarmed in and washed over the coal, and we got out, some of us. The engine room was all panic-struck steam and cockeyed metal. A leg of the Chief stuck up out of the pit under the cylinders, and I tried to pull him free, but it didn't mean anything to him. Finished with engines.

"She was going fast. You felt it on the gratings, and climbed and climbed. Topside you could see it. There was plenty of light for it. She was a day all to herself. The flames bawled mast-high, and the smoke above was red-hot. The chaps were going overside, not waiting for the stuff in her to burst. I let go and jumped before I meant to when she slipped over a few extra degrees, and I hooked on to a raft. Old Con Duffy was the other side of it, still wearing his spectacles, the poor old beggar. He made a face at me as I popped up, and I cheered him on for Paradise. Splashes peppered about us on the water and Con's throat was ripped, and he goggled at me, quite upset, with his mouth open, quite hurt, as if I had done it. . . . Look, what luck . . . a bus, Okeham, just going . . . see you soon, so long."

He made a short run; he swung himself aboard lightly as a dancer, and did not look back.

FOURTEEN

They turned to watch the bus diminish down the road, and as intently as if sure it must pull up in a moment and return for what it had left behind. It rounded a bend; the road was empty.

"Well I'm damned," said Nick.

"He's left his beer," said Stephen.

"I see. So he has. There are three glasses. Count them again. If the extra one wasn't in front of me I'd doubt I was listening to a strange voice a minute ago. Can you hear it now?"

Stephen said he could, fairly well. It was telling them when it stopped about a Con Duffy. That was the name, an old chap in spectacles, holding on to a raft.

"The very man, and it was somewhere towards the eightieth degree north latitude, between everlasting ice and hell's flames. . . . Hadn't we better go home? Come on, let's start before we begin to argue whether the moon is prime Gorgonzola or a phantom."

"He said he'd see us soon."

"Soon, was it? No doubt, and in the same old moonscape. Don't forget your stick. Isn't that it against that seat? Pull yourself together."

74

"I should like to see him again."

"You may. Why not? With God all things are possible."

They mounted leisurely the long ascent to White Stacks, past the gardens of the villas. Stephen paused, at a vantage, to admire the surge of summer in its prime all around. He didn't remember a lovelier season, he remarked. It was a masterpiece, and only that morning did he begin to notice it.

"We've had no time for masterpieces," said his uncle. "Much too busy with bedevilments." Nick himself then took in inaugural bountitude. "It doesn't look as if it had had our worries, does it? It might be trying to persuade us that nothing has happened here, and never will, nothing of importance outside this. Perhaps it is right. Perhaps we are only incidental Bedlamites butting in, and bustling our glorious way out of it. We may learn more about that after dark."

"I wish I knew," said Stephen. "I was thinking just now that the real thing in that fellow's tale wasn't the sea, or the ice, or the ship on fire, or the ugly customers who peppered poor drowning wretches with bullets, but the man himself. You couldn't get a change into that fellow's face. Something about him . . . what was it? It seemed to me he could look on at the last day and not blink. Isn't there a lot in that?"

Nick's smile was kindly, as far as it went. "I suppose there is. It's a way of seeing it if one stands where you do, but I should feel shy if I stood there."

"Try for a moment to stand there."

"No room. You fully occupy it, and always will. But I'll get as near as I can. I'll own up that in a long life I've noticed your sailor is a dependable sort, not infrequent. I've met that fellow before. I came across more than a few of him at the dressing stations, where we tied up human fragments in France. But you never knew that war. Now and then—are you listening?—there's such a fellow in a church pulpit. But what can one do among so many?"

"Nobody knows. Just be himself."

"If you think that holds a chance for us, hang on to it. Hang on. It's better than nothing."

"Isn't it pretty well all? All we can be absolutely certain of?"

"That's a friendly idea. You can't go far wrong with it until you meet—you know—that other sort, and they're round every corner. Now, don't argue with me going uphill, or I'll say you are right. Incipient fatty degeneration on this steep slope makes me glad to agree with even your own father about anything."

Stephen was acutely conscious of the person beside him, this portly relative still nimble and spry though he had been a ship's surgeon under sail; who professed no love for anybody but himself, but was more decent than he pretended to be. Nick was the right companion if only you knew where to find him. Nothing came along but he had a sly word for it, a joke even for his right hand crippled at Ypres; he wouldn't be able to make a blunder in human vitals any more. There was no end to his blithe knowledge, whether of genes and chromo-

76

somes and their conjuring with life's original jelly, or why Lucy had changed from gentleness to gritty antagonism, or how much there was in the legend of lost Atlantis. It was all one to Nick, who made you feel you hadn't been making the best use of your eyes and brain up to now. He made the ordinary seem new and strange. And he was shockingly honest; he could guy himself. All the same, he was isolated, or insulated, not to be touched. You were never nearer to him than his elbow, just as in that moment. The last inch of space between him and another was as inaccessible as the horizon. Must one always be alone, even when beside a man you can trust?

They turned into the approach to hidden White Stacks, and there, too, though on private and secluded ground, Stephen could not rid himself of the queer feeling—it came over him at times—that he was alone in a scene that was transient. They rounded a corner, and saw a figure bent over the rose bushes, with a guard of white fantail pigeons preening themselves about her, and stopped.

"There you are," whispered Nick, "somebody who never has our humorous doubts, and shows no interest in assorted explanations. She tends her garden."

Stephen's mother heard, and looked up. She straightened under the overhead sun, and in that instant Arcadia was not lost but at command. Her appearance was luminous, with her silvery hair and her gray dress, one who was exempt from the heat of mortal noon. Her son was still, and could imagine what he saw was incorporeal, was of the legendary and timeless. As an assurance of present reality she waved her hand to them gaily, and the divine doves cluttered off.

FIFTEEN

On a day of that week, well towards midnight, Stephen was on his way slowly round the landings to his room. White Stacks was returning to its old ways. There had been no air raids for some time. He saw a light under Nick's door, and paused.

He had not spoken more than a dozen words since morning. He ought to commune. The day should be settled into a just perspective with some honest communication before turning in. Bedtime is the hour to make peace with all that is.

His mind, he suspected, was too much at ease. He did not rebuke himself for this. He could not help fancying that he could see breaks in the dun and settled clouds of war; and why should a fellow not let in the good, when it seemed to be begging for admittance? All the same, was it lawful to have a lightened heart? Anyhow, as well as he knew, personal apprehension was not as sharp as before; the soul was working itself free from what had been cramping it. There was a new lightness in the air. The only planes about were friends, and they were in impressive multitudes, and at all hours. The black threat up there had become no more than the memory of a storm that had drifted away to a distant rumbling. Well, though that was all right for him, how did this new mood of faith and hope compare with what was out of sight in the night? He turned the handle of Nick's door.

"Hullo. Do come in." His uncle pushed his book aside. "Not abed yet, and the night so calm? Now what have you to say? Go on. Worry me before sleep with posers only accomplished liars would attempt to answer."

"Not a question, unless it happens to turn up. I only wanted to verify another person before becoming unconscious."

"That means you've been in hiding from the way of the world all day. What have you been doing with yourself?"

"Nothing worth mentioning. That fellow, you know, that sailor we met, he put a figment into my head. I've been trying my hand at some verses. That's all."

"Quite enough, too. Which way did the inspiration take you?"

"Oh, the ballad. Lots of stanzas. Old-fashioned stuff. Something right off the earth, as well as I could raise it."

"Yes? Then don't try it on me at this hour. I've been deep in the particulars of aberration in genius, and I'm not properly receptive, under artificial light. Have at me

79

in the morning, after breakfast, when I'm light-hearted and forgiving. Now get the bottle out of that cupboard. . . . Is that all that's left in it? About enough to toast happy days. Halve it—no, not there—you'll find the glasses behind the microscope."

"I say, you know, is genius aberrant?"

"Of course it is. What would it be if it wasn't?"

"I mean, is it a bit off the center, a sort of lunacy?"

"It's always an eye-opener, isn't it? Always a surprise. It's not like an eggcup on the breakfast table. A dedicated busybody feels a strong lunar pull towards getting what he wants, which of course is us, to direct us to glory, and out pours enough eloquence to make ordinary goings-on of no account. We don't like being disturbed, as a rule, but pretty soon we begin to enjoy the novelty of it. Why not? Anything for a change. Anything to release us from the dreary obligations of common sense."

"That only means Napoleon was a genius, Hitler too, all those conquering anarchists."

"That's what it comes to. It's the authority of superior energy. It rouses our latent good instincts to action. Eloquence sets fire to ignorance, gets the boiler going, and makes power to shift things to an advantage not ours. At the magic call, the mob looks up from the common lot it is grumbling over, as usual, and then off it goes after some Pied Piper, sure the way of the enchanter is the only way. Chucks up the daily round, and is off, and nothing can stop it. Why don't you start a new religion? Think it over. There's always a chance, when there's plenty of yearning about, and nothing to satisfy it but taxes, lap dogs, and the potato plot."

"I see. Then what about Jesus?"

"I thought he was coming along. But he's a puzzle, and I won't go into it. Look at the clock! But do we go his way? I don't. It wouldn't suit my style. Does it suit anybody's? I haven't got the impression that it does, so far, from what I've seen about this week. Have you?"

"That doesn't answer my question."

"Go to blazes. You told me you weren't going to ask any questions."

"Unless one turned up."

It was then they eyed each other sharply. The night itself interrupted them.

"There," said Nick, "there we are. An urgent question has just turned up."

They attended to it. It was the wailing note. For a satisfactory period it had been silent, and there was a hope it had gone for ever. Now once again the warning howl of the siren filled the night without—importunate, undulate, and rending.

Stephen, while waiting for what was to come next, was fixed in acute observation of the details of a room he had known so long that, but for this interruption, he would have accepted with no concern. As it was, everything in it appeared also to be waiting; waiting conspicuously, as he was, and as Nick was, very still.

Nick's face was grim while he eyed a palaeolithic axhead he used as a paperweight, a lump of brown chert that had a story twenty thousand years long since it left the hand of the man who fashioned it to rest at last on Nick's notes for the book he was doing. The little bronze bust of Voltaire, with a faint smile he didn't like, was regarding them both from the center of the mantel-piece; that fellow seemed to know what was going on just then, and it amused him. On either side of Voltaire were the more remarkable of those glistening mineral specimens, of unnamable colors, Nick collected in British Columbia when he was young and preferred to live in wigwams with Indians. What a lot Nick must have seen in his wandering life before the banshee called to him a minute ago! More then he himself would ever see, he supposed. A wad of soot was shaken down the chimney and fell out to the floor.

"I can't hear them moving below," said Stephen.

"No. They've got used to it. They think this won't last long—a last futile kick of the dying beast. We'll stay where we are. What a pity we've finished that bottle."

The wailing, an inordinate length of it, had ceased. The night outside was mysterious with inexplicable noises. The two of them turned to the blacked-out window, as if to question it, but it remained impenetrable and uncommunicative. Their experience of the many varieties of the war's progress in the air was a matter of years, and yet they could not hear in this raid the formid-able throbbing of high bombers. They felt immured and stifled.

"Odd," said Nick. "What's that coming our way again?"

"I don't know. It's rather extra. Sounds to me like a

bundle of iron buckets in flight. I'll put out the light."

Stephen uncovered the window, and together they tried to make out what was going on over Bewley.

"This is a real show," said Nick. "Quite attractive. Those parabolas of tracer bullets are the best I've seen. But what are they doing? Firing off spare ammunition?"

The night into which they peered for meaning was lighted only by a lacework of colored fire in intersecting arcs, and each ascending arc was leisured and graceful, as if for the eye's delight. Now and then White Stacks shook for a reason they could not see, but heard.

"Another advance in knowledge, of course," said Nick, "but what is it? It's here, there's a house burning —it must be pretty near the Mackenzies, too . . . Hullo!"

There was no need to draw attention to what he saw coming their way in that minute. Soaring over the hill, golden in the rays of the searchlights, and so near the earth they were as unbelievable as radiant herald angels, wings outspread, moved a procession of mythical forms, a heavenly host, greeted by numberless upward lines of tracers, a reticulation of prismatic fire, as if mortals were attempting, all unsuccessfully, to cast magic nets aloft to capture celestial messengers so bright.

"What is it? I don't like it," said Stephen. "I'm going down to tell them to get into the cellars."

The radiance of one of the flying objects was suddenly extinguished, and then on the earth, below the point where it had been seen, an incandescent flame shot up to open the sky.

"Yes," said Nick, "you'd better tell them. Stay down yourself."

"You come too," said Stephen.

"Not me. Not at my age. I'll see Hitler and all Germany damned first."

SIXTEEN

The entrance gates to White Stacks were wide open next morning, as if a change of heart had come over Sir Anthony, and he was ready to welcome all comers. The shrubbery and trees screening the house were as pleasant and inviting as usual, and the bees were in the limes. Two wardens, wet and weary on so fine a morning, entered the drive. Several rats scuttled across their path.

"They've been upset," said a warden.

The two men then halted together, and gazed up to the ridge of the hill. A noise in the sky well to the south was growing rapidly into a savage malediction.

"There it is!"

There it was, coming straight at them with the clangor of a tangle of loose ironmongery in flight, a menacing black cross skimming the hill top, its tail a stabbing jet of flame. The wardens watched it narrowly for signs.

"Look out—it's going to . . . No, it's going on."

"Good for another two miles. It will drop beyond the High Street."

They breathed more naturally, and resumed their walk. "That blighter will fall clear of our beat, anyway."

"Where were you when this started?"

"In bed. I thought it was the usual do till I got round to the Mackenzies' place. I heard then what it was. . . . No. Couldn't do anything there. It was all done at once. The blast of these thingamys—doodlebugs you call them—is a flattener."

They emerged from the veiling drive, and were startled by an excess of air and light. Where was White Stacks? The drive ended in vacancy. Their sight went clear across where the house had stood for over two centuries to the trees beyond that hid the lake. There was no house. There was one wall, blackened at the base where a hearth had been. There was that wall, precariously poised, and a mound of rubble before it from which the legs of a piano projected like those of a dead animal, wrong way up; the body of music was all that could be named in the wreckage, except the smell of crumbled plaster, and the buzz of flies. They took a full minute to believe what was before them.

"What's happened to the Gales? They must have had one to themselves."

"Haven't heard. There's no tally of last night yet. It will take some reckoning up, if ever it can be counted.

. . . My oath, we all came to somewhere new last night, and where are we?"

"The likes of this will have to be paid for."

"Paid for. Paid for. How? It's gone."

SEVENTEEN

The sergeant of the firewardens, at the entrance to Bewley Hospital, a gray-haired veteran, was alert to the stretch of anxiety. With the scatter of people who were near, his face was upturned to the sky. They had been warned. More violence was flying towards them. It would burst in the next few minutes and where would it drop? The sergeant had doffed his helmet to scan the brilliant vault nearer the meridian; and the vault was of the kind of blue that once had its place in the innocence of a shepherd's idyll. The array of tokens of battles of other years, that decorated the sergeant's tunic, suggested that the figure of the fateful skeleton with the poised dart in plain sight and striding fast towards him would be incidental to his day's work; that he was at home in scenes that would panic the multitude.

The senior medical officer approached to pass through the gates, his Malacca cane under his arm, and his head bowed. He was altogether too leisurely and holiday-like, the sergeant thought, for such intimidating sunshine.

"The alert has sounded, sir."

"I heard. I heard." The surgeon stepped back graciously to allow a woman to pass who was hurrying along with a perambulator and two infants.

"It is rarely silent," he added. "It means we want you men all the time."

"We're here, sir."

The surgeon, fumbling at a cord, put up his eyeglass for a steady survey of the little white clouds afloat in the southern blue. He let his glass fall. "Nothing seems to be coming our way yet. Perhaps some other sector is catching it. And I must say you look as if you ought to be hardened to this sort of thing."

"Not at all, sir. Nobody is."

"Nobody is."

"In the old front line, sir, we had to take it, off and on like. Now," he added plaintively, "It's everywhere, and never stops."

The surgeon nodded. His apparent indifference to immediate peril brought the sergeant's interest down from the sky. The old soldier was compelled instead to continued rigid attention in an irksome attitude.

"Where were you in the other war?" The doctor's amiable concern was only that of a fellow-sufferer, and he was in no hurry.

"From Mons to Arras, sir."

"What! All that time without the knockout? Then you have nothing to worry about. You must wear a magic shirt."

"Not at all, sir. I've had some. But if I said these 'ere newfangled buzz bombs didn't scare me cold I'd be a holy liar."

"Quite. And so say all of us. Um. Ah. A thought recurs. What was it the trenches used to be called? You must have heard it when on leave. The place of honor. Bear in mind that honor this morning takes in the cradles, the hospital wards, and the pubs. Everybody shares it. I wonder what becomes of it then." He touched the path about with his cane, as if looking unhopefully for a strayed and weakened virtue. He looked up at his man. "No matter. You'll know a little before the patients when one of the brutes is about to dive on us."

"Yessir."

The surgeon went on, and the guardian at the gate eyed his bent and studious back. "Very good, Doctor bloomin' Pickles, sir, we'll double up," he promised the air, "if standing on our cold feet."

Within the hospital the air was cool. The warning had been heard there, of course, but the only sign of alarm had been a trifling pause in whatever its people were doing, and an exchange of glances across its wards. There being no other refuge for its people, they must wait where they were for what might come; so it kept its air of a sanctuary of peace, immune from disturbance through an increased stress of storm without. Its staff on duty moved blithely and soothingly as if the morning were pleasant and crisis had no power to distort mortal bodies. A workman trundled through a corridor a trolley laden with anonymous rubbish in which only yesterday's

88

plaster and broken glass were evident. He passed as un-remarked as the old lady taking in, as usual, her morning tribute of roses. Her bouquet was an assurance of affection. His load of rubbish was customary. A flying monster had fallen the day before into a near street, and its blast had ruined hospital accommodation, for the use of which it had brought immediate need.

Two nurses stood in the way of the trolley, and one of them did not see it, for her hands were covering her eyes. She was guided aside by her consoling colleague, who whispered urgently, "Hush. Here comes Dr. Pickles." The girl made sure of this with a quick glance, and then darted into a side corridor to hide her face.

"Gladys in trouble this morning?" asked the surgeon.

"No, sir. Well, it's a patient. It's a young woman Gladys knew. She was a neighbor and she was brought in here after one of the things fell in Woodland Terrace, which you'll remember. She was forever asking Gladys day and night whether her family was all right, and Gladys daren't tell her. The upset here when the thing fell yesterday was too much for her, and this morning . . . "

"Yes, yes. The finishing touch. You'd better tell Gladys she is now relieved of the duty to confess that her friend's family is not all right. So much is gained."

"Oh, Dr. Pickles!" But he was on his way.

He stood for a moment by the door of his room, a hand upon the catch of it. He raised his monocle to peer down the long vista of the ward beyond. At its far end was the Matron, gravely observing a patient. A few visitors were with her. He recognized Sir Anthony Gale in the group, and wondered why he was there. He knew the man, but did not care greatly for that important and peremptory person. Sir Anthony in this place? Gale? He seemed to remember the name, as a recent casualty. Gale?

Without further speculation he entered his own place. He hoped the Matron had not seen him. Solitude for five minutes, and no urgency anywhere about anything, no scattering sudden outburst, especially the raucous downfall of glass, no cries for help, no consultation over a problem, forced on him without notice, and not to be solved without all knowledge; and his knowledge was less than that, somewhat. He supposed this was weariness in him. Getting too old for it. If only he were sixty again!

He couldn't help doubting that two long wars in one lifetime was overdoing honor. Rather too much of it for the ordinary heart. The mortal frame was not made for the drive of so many frantic years. There was a job for him, in the next hour, and it was no better than trying to filch a body from the mortuary—bomb splinters that had just missed cutting the thin-spun thread, and when he touched them, would they click? Too much of it, trying to keep life on the move in the never-ending output of mutilations by hate; for hate never tires. He took a bottle from a private store of cordials, considered its label briefly, noted what was left of its contents, and returned it to its place.

At the far end of the ward, with the Matron and Sir

Anthony, was Lucy. She was too insignificant a figure for Dr. Pickles to have noticed. She was contemplating Stephen, from the foot of his bed, and he was far away. She had kissed his forehead, but he was nowhere near her. She meditated in the silence.

—How far away? Nobody could tell her. Nobody knew. It was no good asking. He was out of reach. Stephen! Look at me. Do you know what has happened to us? All's gone. Oh, Steve! All's gone. We shan't stand on the stairs again, listening. There will be no music from Mother's room any more, the dear darling. Silence. Stephen, don't keep so far off. Look, it's me. Here I am. I want you more than ever. He doesn't remember, does he? No, it isn't that. He never kept mean little things in mind. It was my fault, Stephen. It was only the war. No more than the war. War and its misery. It hurt. Didn't it hurt you? You never said, did you? Stephen. My dear Steve.

Not a sign. Nothing. Is the distance past all contriving? Past all contriving. Nothing of the ordinary is left of him, only the dear boy's untidy hair on the pillow. Not a puzzling thought on his forehead. All smoothed out. Not the least smile to pretend he wasn't taking it seriously. Queer. There's firm purpose in that chin. She had never noticed it before. What purpose? The stern lines of his calmness, and his eyes shutting her out, and his hawklike nose gone white, recalled something. She knew. It was that picture of his namesake, after the stoning. Finished. Thrown out.

He would not think hardly of her, wherever he was

now. No victim of this war could think badly of her, could they? Do good men always have that look of indifference when cruelty has done its worst? Does the mind at rest on what it knows bring those lines of mastery about the mouth without meaning to? It wouldn't be condemnation, would it? Yet they are fixed and stern. They rebuke those who would speak to them again, say the right thing, when wrong has been done, when words won't do any more. O God, let him open his eyes, let him see me here. All would be well. Stephen, tell us something from where you are. Say this cruel world does not matter, only that. Say it doesn't matter. Say only that. Give me patience with it all.—

She turned abruptly to her father at some whispered converse she overheard. "What did the Matron say? What did she say?"

Sir Anthony slowly shook his head. "Nothing. There has been no change in him since he came in. That is all. We can do no good here. We had better go."

The Matron was watching Sir Anthony professionally. She had the idea that if this had happened to her it would have been the end, or as near as didn't matter. It was one more astonishing instance of what body and soul could suffer without breaking. You had to see it to believe it. He must be of bronze. He stood looking at his only son, who might be dying, as if at a crusader's image in a niche.

Sir Anthony made to go. "Thank you, madam. You will give him help that we cannot give. Thank you."

He turned away, blundering without apology into a

nurse who was in attendance. He thought vaguely that he wasn't taking this the right way, or perhaps he had gone dead inside and didn't feel it. It might be better so. There is no help in standing and staring at wreckage. This might have to be paid for later; payment deferred. "Come, my girl. There is something still to be done. We will go and do it. It will carry us along."

The Matron slowly followed as far as Dr. Pickles' room, for she knew he was within. She told the doctor, after a desultory consultation, that Sir Anthony Gale had just left the hospital.

"I saw him with you. Why?"

"A casualty. His son."

"I seemed to remember the name among many. In the confusion I did not connect it with the big house. What happened?"

"The house was destroyed."

"What's that? What? Who was there?"

"Lady Gale, her son, and her brother. She was with her son and the maid in the cellars. When things grew worse that night the son went up to get his uncle to join them. His mother followed, so the maid says, because she thought she could better persuade her brother. It happened then. I thought everybody knew."

"I didn't know."

"But wasn't Dr. Tregarthen a friend of yours?"

"He was. We were together at St. Thomas's, and in Flanders and . . . Killed, you say?"

"Yes."

The Matron methodically gathered up some scattered

documents, scanning a sheet here and there for a desired particular. Prompted by an outburst of noise urgent and doleful, she shuffled the sheets together in a hurry and made for the door. "The warning again," she remarked.

Dr. Pickles did not move. He might not have heard. He sat regarding his desk as if it ought to have hidden somewhere about it the clue to a matter of the first importance, and he had that moment given up hope of ever finding it. It had gone. Then he rose awkwardly, still abstracted, his gaze still downward on the unrelenting aspect of his desk with its spread of that day's injunctions. He was weighing in his hand, absent-mindedly, a paperweight. This object he presently examined curiously, as though unsure of his first intent with it. He replaced it delicately.

"So there we are," he said to himself. "No more Tregarthen. Now when I cannot see the gist of it, who is there to tell me?"

EIGHTEEN

Night fell, and deepened, and the keeper of the watch at Bewley's hospital gates, within which Stephen Gale was left to his possible dreaming, sauntered along to the end

94

of the boundary wall, followed at a respectful distance by a dog he did not know was there.

The night, too, for that patch of war, was tranced and dreamlike. The automata of havoc were in flight, but were thankfully at a good height, and hurtling towards other people. The sentry was expecting his relief, and would welcome it. Nobody was in sight. He was beginning to fancy that he was forgotten, that he was far on the outside of the bustle and stir, that he might never see a pal again. So reserved were the precincts of his vigilance that the dubious and empty road, without a movement in it either way as far as he could see, and the shapes of the trees and houses, weird in moonlight filtering faintly through unbroken cloud, gave him the uneasy notion that all about him brooded on an event to come, and perhaps soon, and was abandoned to its fate.

Was the curtain about to shoot up, and the lights? He hoped not. If his relief would only turn up, he could make himself scarce with fair luck.

At the end of the wall he paused close to a bus stop. It gave the sentry the impression that it had seen its last bus. Near it, under a hornbeam, was that old granite horsetrough: "In memory of the Horses fallen in the South African War, 1900–2."

He looked north, watching the reflection of the flames of a new fire Londonwards pulsing on the cloud-ceiling. That was the fifth in sight, not counting the flashes. He had given up counting the flashes. That new blaze wasn't too small, either. It would be near Bermondsey. The swine were keeping it up proper.

Here came another. The snarling of the brute was low in the overhead pallor, but not too low. That thing would miss Bewley by a sufficient distance. It would be only another flash. The dog close behind him rumbled deep disapproval of an enemy at hand, not daring to bark.

"Hullo," exclaimed the sentry, turning round. "What's the matter with you? What are you doing here?"

He stooped to pat and reassure the vagrant. "Don't you like it?" The dog still shivered, and growled after the threat retreating. It came up against the man, as there had been no rebuke. At the sentry's feet he squatted, assuming that safety was found and he could rest. The man, still bent over the stray, twisted his face upwards, attentive to duty while showing one more of the humble and homeless that he fully sympathized. He could hear another horror on its way, and this one was much lower, and it was heading for them.

Its snarling abruptly ceased. Here was the end of its flight. It was curving over in its silent plunge. "Now for it," he muttered to the dog, and stretched full length on the ground.

The burst jolted him, and in a vivid dispersion of obscurity the treetops and chimney pots across the road leaped high with inky distinction against brilliance, and vanished again instantly. The dog barked valiantly.

"Withy Bottom got that one. Do you know anybody there?" said the man to the dog.

That area of battle relapsed into neutrality. For a while there was no sound till the sentry picked up, very far off, a faint humming in the sky. That one was all right. One of ours. A bonny night-fighter up there was on his way. Even the dog knew he need not notice it, for the man's demeanor over him was indolent.

The hospital of the sentry's particular care, after the shock and the burst of light, relapsed again and was lost in the common shadow of the immemorial earth. The man who was watching over it did not look that way. He gave it no thought. He could see his relief approaching. All that the building behind him, hidden in trees, had known of compassion and healing, of agony and courage, of grief and hope, was dissolved into night and forgetfulness. It was no more than one of the ambiguous reminders of a life gone by, that raise no more than a sigh in the living present.

"What, Bert, you're late. I was giving you up. Didn't your old woman want to let you out tonight?"

NINETEEN

In the heavens high over the hospital—or thereabouts—where an airplane was making a friendly sound, its guiding genius knew little of what was below him in the void. He could not see the earth. He was above the clouds. Bewley to him was but a name. He was in his war dress, and so his mother would have hesitated over his identity. While questing for trouble, he was leveled to the universal martial type.

It was only when down below on his feet, with his messmates about him, that he became individual, and was The Kid; for he had gone straight into the air, as it were, from a school desk. He had not the appearance, while waiting the call to action, of an experienced man-at-arms. Without his battle accouterment he seemed too fresh and diffident to hold a warrant to set out, at the summons, to face the ultimate. Of course, his once free curls had been shortened to a ginger crispness, but only the years could improve the juvenile blob of his nose, and settle firmly the soft moist pink of his lips. There were his eyes and jaw, and they did hint, to the wary, that he might prove a difficult child, if upset.

He had yet to learn more fully, while below on the earth, what life is like beyond airdromes. He had not had the time for it. Girls, to him—and he had noticed them about, sometimes closely—were less welcome than a spare part seen in the moment of necessity. He preferred speculating over the possibilities in machines to discovering the drift and beauty in books. He never contributed to the tales passed round of the quality and numbers of the flying foe; this for him was a private matter, as he had seen several of the enemy go down, or at least make a lot of comforting smoke, whereas his own little winged beauty behaved precisely as he had prompted her; and what more would you want? He was attentive, but silent, while listening to gossip about the best dodges to avoid the vulgar hazards which issued gratuitously from headquarters and air-marshals and other powers, remote but absolute; and he had no more than a friendly smile, to show he was doing his best to be sociable, when he was told allusively of delightful mitigation to be found, and near by, when a chap wished, before he passed out, to push war off his mind during a brief interlude of simple joy.

He was also known at times, to those who admired his native skill yet hoped it would not be the end of him too soon, as Jimmy the Daft, to distinguish him from several other more knowing Jimmies. For he was not the one to recognize risks and accept them boldly like a man. He was but lightly aware of lurking peril, and did not flatter it with calculating attention. He had all the luck. His chosen place was on high, where self was undistracted by the fussiness of law and order. The air was his element, and his faith aloft was perfect that he and his machine were one body, a faith natural to eager and happy simplicity. Up there, when trespassers were met with, they were out of place, and his lawful prey. He was as easy on the aerial tides as a bird. He came to himself when at play with his machine. Bright vacancy supported his dreams of the future.

It was supporting him in the minute over Bewley when the sentry and the dog caught the sound of his presence aloft. He was well above the ceiling of cloud, alone, at large, and had all a universe in clear moonlight to himself. He could see the bright side of things. He was solitary in infinitude. He had one bond with earth, the tiny voice in his headphones of a chap somewhere down under, in a room furnished with antennas sensitive to any distant movement of the foe; and so he had notice in advance, when he happened to be the right man for it. He is flying at this moment as a footnote, across this page of some brief annals of his period, unaware that down below were listeners who knew he was up there, unseen but protective; and he will pass over and beyond fairly soon. He could see nothing under him but cloud, and so the neighborhood of Bewley to him was the surface of a bright and boundless ocean, all snowy billows, and all arrested in a last undulation, flowing no more, billows frozen by the cold light of the moon. No movement showed in that luminous sea of arctic white but the magnified shadow of his own outspread wings.

In so spacious a solitude the small voice spoke to him, and it was only as if the call to immediate action was his personal intuitive warning of the presence of the enemy. He dived into the white surge, which engulfed him and his shadow, and presently shot into the lower dark. There, nearer to earth, was the intrusive dragon below him, on a London course, and marked by its jetting flame. His heart whooped. He dropped to meet the monster to blow out its flame, letting go with his guns when almost on it.

Its flame went out. He had but a falcon's span in which to swerve and avoid. His unknown familiar deep in a subterranean office heard his mild response: "I gottim."

TWENTY

The rattle of his guns, with the abrupt extinction of a comet they were watching streak athwart the night, surprised two men standing outside the entrance to a family air-raid shelter in a suburban garden. They flung themselves to the grass.

"Come down out of it," cried a woman from underground, alarmed by the sound of near gunfire. "What are you waiting up there for? The hearse?"

The explosion answered her. She was with them, frightened and disarrayed, as they scrambled to their feet. One of them chuckled, and anger followed her fear.

"Lovely weather for watching it, ain't it? So what's this hole for?"

"Don't worry, Ma. It was only a rotten miss."

"It's not enough to have the boys in it, is it? You got to have a bit of a gamble for sport." Her voice weakened. "Doesn't it matter?"

"It's kept in mind, sweetheart. Down you go before the next beauty pops over."

She was overstressed, while looking round the night. "Some poor souls caught it then. Where was it?"

"The allotments. Up went the vegetables. And after all the work they've had out of me."

"Damn the vegetables." She fumbled hastily with her hair.

"You'll think different come Sunday dinnertime. Get below, Mother. Another on its way now."

They stooped in turn to enter a mound covered with galvanized iron. Ten earthen steps led down to a rectangular cave lit by a small electric bulb, a glow so feeble that its continuance was in doubt. Its light but picked out angles of the struts and beams that gave security to walls of clay. Bunks were fitted in recesses beyond the struts. Two bundles on those inner shelves, out of the reach of the light, were children asleep. A shawled figure sat huddled on a box, in the pose of Atropos, her gray hair disheveled and hiding her face as she bent over to read the floor. She raised her head inquiringly at them as they entered, as if to messengers unlikely to have the news for which she had long waited.

"Has the Kaiser given in?" she asked.

The inattention and silence of the other three told her that this latest struggle outside with the bugbear had failed again. She resumed her steady reading of the floor at her feet. Her daughter went over to her and adjusted a shawl to indifferent shoulders, and then huddled on a neighboring box, as if to understudy her mother's part.

"That was a queer do," said the younger of the men.

"We were there to see it, son. Tackled by a night-flier. That's a job he can have all to himself. If he had hit its nose instead of its tail, eh?"

"He wouldn't have known it."

"It might have been our young Ted," said the younger woman.

"More likely it wasn't. We won't speculate," said the elder man. "Anything goes, while we wait here, and what do we know? I'll have a look at those potatoes come morning."

"I hope the boy who shot it down got away," said his wife. "Did he?"

"The light wasn't too good," said her man. "You might as well ask Grandma."

Grandma lifted her head at her name, and spoke. She said, "Fippence for the lot of it." She added, less mysteriously, "When are we going home?"

They did not tell her. They were attending to the approach of another missile.

"Time to be off, Dad," said the younger man, when its noise faded out. "If I wait for the all clear it might be Christmas. I got to get to Sally and the nipper." He adjusted his helmet, and made to ascend.

"Take the left road, Joe. Better make for Southwark Bridge. The other way's a riot. Most of St. Saviour's Church isn't shifted off it yet."

Joe mounted a bicycle. The clouds were breaking up. The moon looked down on him through a clear oriel of sky. His ride was in a deserted land, but there were interludes where the eruption of an automaton had assembled a rescue party at a gap in the houses, with ambulances waiting close to the wreckage. Once he had to dismount and carry his bicycle over a tangle of fire hose

hissing random fountains, the water in the road as tremulous and bloody as the flames roaring out of roof and
windows. He went by these scenes of activity as speedily
as he could, asking no questions, for his own place in
war was elsewhere, and what he saw were but the customary wayside incidents in a changed prospect of existence, to be accepted with the rations and the casualty
lists.

TWENTY-ONE

He pedaled at speed over Southwark Bridge, and did not
glance at the river. Its polished silver was immaculate. It
retained no mark of its ancient use, except the black
shadows of its warehouses. The Thames seemingly had
entered a future Londoners did not share.

He turned into Cannon Street, and continued with his
eyes to the road round the cathedral. There, as ever, its
mass lifted in buoyant ascendancy, but he took the noble
landmark as he did the sky and the moon, and as he
would the sun on the morrow, without a thought. There
St. Paul's was, so he knew his way, though that night it
ruled in lonely majesty over a waste as silent as a king-
dom lost in ages forgotten. Around it, to a dreamlike distance, fugitive moonlight changed isolated jags of ruin

into specters, gaunt and pallid, all that remained standing of a labyrinth of ancient streets in which men once had been busy in traditional confidence of purpose. They had vanished, they and their streets, and their purpose. In the midst of that phantom solitude, the abiding cross surmounting the cathedral's mass was occasionally as bright as a beacon, though nobody was there to see it, and in desolation it was the sole promise of the continuity of good.

He went on round the occupying landmark, and presently leaned his bicycle in a narrow way against a wall so deep in shadow that it was as indistinct as antiquity. He fumbled about the wall, a portion of it moved inwards to his touch, and he passed through it. With outstretched fingers he felt his way down a stone stairway, and entered what, in a feeble glow of no visible source, could have been a medieval crypt. That indeed is what it was, as if one of the living had chanced on a lost entrance to where some of the English had been asleep since the earlier London of their day was dust. Their remains, shrouded and anonymous under the low vaulting, in a feeble light, appeared to have lost centuries ago all concern with what men were doing in the streets. He stepped between the forms, and found two he sought, and touched one. She sat up instantly, wide-eyed in either wonder or fear, and resurrection then seemed as simple as being born.

"Joe!"

"Right enough, Sally, it's me."

"Oh, Joe! How . . . are you all right?"

"All right for ten days."

Their infant stirred, and wailed. Its father lifted it, and it stretched without opening its eyes, and loosened again into sleep.

"That's the best noise I've heard in months," said the man on leave.

TWENTY-TWO

Straight up from the sleepers in the medieval crypt, but out of sight in the sky, the night-fighter turned back, southeast for Kent. The lucid illimitable vault, midway in which he floated, accompanied by clouds like rafts of imponderable iron, told him of something unknown to the wardens and sentries down below in the streets; he could see that the earth had heaved over so far towards another day that dawn was nearing them.

He could read little that was in the deep below him. The greatest of maritime cities was nebulous, its only plain fact the serpenting Thames, a silver riband sectioned straight under him by black filaments, its bridges.

It was the river which proved his place in the sky, as once it advised his ancestors that they had found the right place on which to settle down, and where afterwards, keeping faith with their children, they prospered the venture; for that reason, there that night he was. The great loop of the river downstream, formed by the reaches of Limehouse, Greenwich, and Blackwall, was outlined for the airman's eye in a bright shape, an unmistakable shape, as if it were London's heart, to keep pulsing the tides of life, sustaining hope in an original purpose; and it was also his sure bearing for his base, where he was about due.

He could see, at his altitude, that the farthermost clouds, ranged level along the eastern base of the celestial vault, just over the perilous estuary that is the portal to London, were distinguished by keels of gold; and up from the horizon came the first clear promise of a dominant radiance. Time, he could have surmised, is, in one sense, the slow compulsion of light.

TWENTY-THREE

The earth, still turning, presently lifted the sun high enough to peer through the windows of the Fitzgerald Ward of Bewley Hospital. There, at first, it so distinguished the flowers on the sills within that the truth about them was gaily transparent. Then the waxed floor boards were responsive as day crossed the room to show Stephen Gale kept to his pose of the ageless crusader.

A nurse in blue and white, who entered the ward as if quickened by the coming of morning after a night of blackout and alarms, was caught in a beam from a window, and turned in it to acknowledge the blithe innocence of this young hour just entering dire war with flowers. She did not know that, poised as she was in brightness, she was one with it. Dr. Pickles, leaving his room in answer to an urgent summons, was checked in his purpose when he saw Nurse Bridget standing there, trim and seemly, and he became aware, while looking at her, as an elderly understanding male, that he had never been, and would never be, as successful in life as that; and then went off to his saving task with irrational regret for the years irrevocably lost, somewhere, between him and the prime.

Stephen slept as before, calm in his dreaming, perhaps of what has been, perhaps of what might be. A venerable hospital attendant went past him carrying a flimsy red screen, which he erected about a cot on the opposite side of the ward; and then departed with bowed head and pendent beard, drearily, as if this business of shutting another of them out of the world, especially when morning is so fresh, should be stopped, or he would smash his hourglass and drop his scythe.

The patient in the bed next to Stephen sat up and frowned, while watching the sign of finality going about an unknown patient. He turned to his neighbor and made a comment, suitably wry. Stephen, however, remained indifferent. The man kept his frown, but the wryness went from his lips as he gave Stephen closer attention. Could it be? Wasn't this the young fellow who told him the way to Okeham? Outside the pub down the road, the pub with the funny name? The Adam and Eve, wasn't it?

That was the chap. Sure of it. His jib gave him away. Was he a war casualty? And come to think of it, there couldn't be two jibs of the same cut in town on the same day. It wouldn't be real. When they yarned outside the pub—he'd forgotten when—it seemed to him the young 'un was ignorant enough to spit to windward. The milk was on his mouth. All the same, he had the proper articles in his make-up. He was the sort of fellow that gets pushed aboard a ship, and out he goes because the home part is too small for his larks. He was good enough to be standing by when it is blowing up for a black night. Anybody could see it now. He was done to rights in handsome marble.

The nurse approached. "Miss Bridget, I want you," said the man.

She stood near, near enough to hear him guardedly, and there was less of cheerful brightness about her, for she knew this patient's speech could be that of a seaman at liberty.

"Now what is it, Mr. McLuckie?"

He indicated Stephen. "How long's he been here?"

"You are beginning to notice things. We shall be able to let you out quite soon, I hope. He was here before you were."

"Was he, and all! Who is he, and what got him?"

"You had better wait till he is able to tell you—that is, if he wants to tell you."

"He's not looking as if he would soon feel up to it, is he? I can't say you've touched him up to be a good speaking likeness, not yet. He used to laugh. I met him once before, so I know."

"You do? You know him? Well, if what you know of him were of help to us, how nice that would be!"

"The devil it would! And I thought today was set fair. I'd like to hear what I've done this morning, so far, to make you as sharp as a knife on a cold day. It's not right, not if you want me fit to pass muster. How can it put me on my legs to be told I'm nearly ready to leave you?"

He could see, so far from relenting with her usual good humor, that she was not listening. Her concern went over him to the man in the bed beyond. He turned his eyes indolently to that profile in its alabaster composure, and then regarded her again, and understood that nothing he could say would detach such a woman's interest from what was next door. She went swiftly round to Stephen and bent over him in close scrutiny.

"Is he coming round?" asked the patient behind her. She did not say.

"Tell you what," advised the sailor. "Give him one of your best. That's the thing to do. If that doesn't pull him round, he's gone."

She wheeled in annoyance, but dignity mastered impulse, helped by a novice down the ward. The novice, she noticed, was at a window staring up at the meridian as anxiously as if the trumpet announcing judgment were about to be thrust through the sky. She called sharply to the girl to come to her.

"Never do that, Maggie," she whispered. "It worries those unable to move. We shall know soon enough when anything is coming. Go help to bring in their breakfasts."

Nurse Bridget mused, with cheeks more richly tinctured than a trifle should evoke, when again she turned to Stephen, for she had suspected in him signs of revival. And there indeed he was, just sitting up, intent on nothing, and pointing sternly at what he could see there—but all she saw there was, as before, a lamp in suspension.

He relaxed and surveyed the ward. His eyes encountered hers, and for a moment were fixed in astonishment and incredulity, and in some fear, too, or so she fancied in disquiet; for he seemed to see plainly in her face a fault so secret that the mirror had never shown it to her.

He evaded her regard, which he did not appear to want, and discovered next to him the fixed eyes of the sailor, and to him cried out in delighted hail. He then sank back into his former world, as if he had found in this one, and too soon, more than he had the strength to meet.

The nurse's voice, when next she spoke to the sailor, was without acerbity. "Do you think he saw us? You say you have met him, but he has never seen me."

The sailor stroked his nose. "Can't say, Miss Bridget. He saw something, but God knows what we see when we're not where we think we are."

TWENTY-FOUR

Stephen, in fact, just before he looked round, was at sea.
He was afloat in an open boat. He knew that boat. It
was the same boat, grown large, that he used to push out
on the lake, blue outside and white within to show the
sea and the sun had stained it, so his mother said. He
didn't know how it came to be where it was, and didn't
ask. He must have been afloat for years and years. He
didn't know how long. Sailing through empty space very
likely. He remembered nothing of it. He eased the sheet
a little.

The sun was blazing straight down from overhead,
and the boat's boards had soaked it in. A bright shine in
a silence as wide as the sky made him as happy as he was
when a child, and alone. The boat was as old as the early
days. The flat of the sea was shot-silk, and right to the
bottom it was as thin as air. Shoals of fishes, red and
blue, and striped in purple and silver, swam slowly alongside, keeping up with the boat, on the same course,
friendly fashion. No shadows were left. They had sailed
clear of all that. It was full day here, always, and no mistakes anywhere, unless made.

The Sailor was in the bows, on the lookout. It was surprising how that man's rags held up on him. It must have been a long voyage. "What land is that?" asked Stephen.

"Cape Flyaway," said the Sailor. "Now you see it, and now you don't."

"Shall we land there?"

"What's it for, if we can keep it in sight?"

They kept it in sight. They were favored. "I've never known this happen before," said the Sailor. "It never does this for me, so it must be for you."

"Who lives there?"

"Nobody lives there. There it is, as it was when Noah missed it. Mind your eye ashore, all the same, or you'll start something you can't belay, and sorry you'll be. It has happened before. Lee, o! Put her alongside that rock. She'll do. Jump for it."

Stephen jumped, and he was there, as easy as a goat. It was the best place he had ever seen. He looked about him. This was where he had always wanted to be. He couldn't keep his eyes from roving over the luck of it. He was going to tell the Sailor to come ashore, that they had found the right coast, and turned about to do it.

There was no Sailor, and no boat. The boat was a speck on the skyline, and the only speck.

He had it to himself, and was sorry. He wanted to share this good thing. That Sailor was the right sort, and deserved it. Now he had to do the best he could for himself in a land he didn't know, where nobody lived. A lizard all in grass-green enamel raised itself on its arms to inspect him, and he picked it up, and it was a handful.

Its eyes were garnets, and its throat was slowly pulsing as it watched him. "Mind your eye," it said in a deep voice heavier than itself, while its throat moved but not its mouth. Stephen kindly set it back on its rock, and it stayed there, watching him.

The lizard had only one thing to say, and he couldn't stand all day on a rock with the tide rising, listening to it, so he moved off inland. As he went along, he became more and more certain that he knew this land. He had seen it before. It was very like the picture in one of the big books he used to open on the carpet before he could read without help. That was why the place knew him. It knew he had come at last. It knew he was wondering what would happen next, though there was nobody to warn what he mustn't do, no flaming sword and that sort of thing out of a book, so there was nothing to worry him. At the same time, he felt he was being watched. The palm trees bent over him to see him go by. And if there was never the flicker of a movement anywhere, and he couldn't hear a whisper, yet as he turned the corners he knew he was only not just sharp enough to catch sight of things as they slipped behind trees. The Sailor was wrong. Something did live here, though it had no shape.

There was no harm in it. It was only on guard against the wrong sort of trespasser. He could go on as he liked. He was springy. He sang to himself. He could float upwards, or very nearly. Feeling like this, he could go as far as world without end. The sky here never grew storms. There was nothing to remember to make tomorrow look sorry it had to come.

He came to the best corner of all, and stood to take it in. Among other fine things there, he saw that what he had to do when he wanted to be sure that everything was as it should be, was to empty his head of last week, of everything, and keep quiet, and be very still like this. The little things about him were as important as the sky. They had meaning. The stars were no brighter than those leaves he had just shoved aside, as they hung between his nose and the outlook. He had struck them, but they were figures in emerald, topaz, and ruby, out of reach of the best words of the best poets. He was seeing the world as he saw it once, he didn't know when. It was the world before the deluge, before all the upsets, and it was his, and he could choose for himself.

It was in that very moment, or soon after, that it happened. He wasn't sure, as he stood there, which way he should go, as all ways were his, or he thought they were. It made no difference which way his choice went, or so he believed.

Which path should he take? He looked about him. There, at the back of him, was one running into the woods. It surprised him that he had not seen it before. Had it been there from the start? It might be keeping something from him, it had such a touch of secrecy. It was a shadow of the night, and the first he had noticed since he came ashore. He ought to find out to what it led in so free a place. No warning was against it. He couldn't see any. There was nothing against it, only a doubt in his own head; and that, he knew, was fear holding him back from what he wanted to do. If danger was on the path, so much the better on a day like this.

He took it. It was wild with brambles, and he had not known they grew there. They resisted him. The thorns were no better than a warning to keep out. They fixed his purpose. The worse the trouble, the more the curiosity, and he had it. He ought to find out what it was he wanted to know.

Unexpectedly he was released into a clearing in the full sun. Nobody else had been that way in the forest for he couldn't tell how long. It was abandoned where memory was lost. The trees stood around brooding over the loneliness of that clearing. They stood off, as if they feared to come nearer to a hut standing in the center. It looked no better than world's end, after all. He had come to it so soon. It was as close at hand as a day's march from where he started.

A shadow drifted between him and the sun, and chills with it, and he kept under the trees. Some sad recollection was here, and it affected even sunlight. The trees felt it, and he felt it.

He was drawn over slowly to the forlorn dwelling. He wanted to learn the truth, if any was left. The hut had no door. A darkness was within that no morning would ever move, so at first he saw only spiders and slippery things, because in the stillness they shot fast across the floor. Then he saw a hammock was hanging on the far side. Somebody was in it.

He crossed the floor to it because he must, as he had come. A woman was in the hammock. There would have been loveliness in her abundant chestnut hair but for the rest of her. He shut his eyes at the sight of hers, which were worse than open on his. The last day she saw was long ago, before the seasons had names.

TWENTY-FIVE

That was when Stephen sat up at Bewley, and looked round his hospital ward for help. He sank back, tired out. He came to again, but was in another country.

The sun was not in that land. It had light, neither of the sun nor the moon, and what was worse it was going out, what there was of it. This other land was as sere and sad as the bygone. Nothing he knew was in sight but an empty road. It was the road home. He didn't know why it was the road home, but he knew it. He would go home.

At last the light was gone, but the road was under his feet. He plodded on. He must get out of this. He must go on to what he knew, to where there were camps, and friends. He was getting on already, because far off he could see a new day on its way. Ahead of him was a low illuminated arc in the night, and he soon knew where. It was home. High in the glare of it floated a shape he knew. The dome of St. Paul's told him he was getting back again, and just in time. He could hear singing. Midnight had struck. A new year had begun, and they were giving it fireworks and chorus.

There was a night when he was there with Lucy. They went to see the fun. She wouldn't be here tonight. He had come to another age, though the same people were about, as well as he could see them. He couldn't see them very well. Their shapes were thin and flitting, like thoughts. You would expect that when old things had passed away, and the great age was beginning anew. He spoke to none of the shadows about him, for perhaps they spoke another language in the year they had come to.

Around St. Paul's was the fun of the fair, booth after booth, and the lions, the bearded woman, the fortune tellers, and the contortionists and the evening papers, carrying on the same old game about the old place, though tonight was in an age not yet come, not by many new thanksgivings. The show was all lit up in a fitful light that you would have said had gone out long ago, gone like great-grandfather. But there it was, all the light they had; the same wretched naphtha flares still spluttered and roared. It was their only help, though its smoky trickiness had let down all the dead.

He'd never squeeze into that crowd. The road was packed tight. But he found no trouble in it, though, no trouble at all. The crowd had no push in it. It had no more bones than are ever found in shadows. The crowd

118

was only numberless faces drifting along before the flickering lamps of the great fair, gaping up at the showmen, taking in whatever was shouted at them; faces as many as the waves of a stream flowing slowly under the high cliffs of a city of the night, pink and vacant faces bobbing along ever forward like bubbles. It was a one-way street. They were all going the same way home, and they were as silent as the drift of history, and he was going with them. He could not get lost, moving like this with the course of events.

Uneasiness took him, though he was home again. He suspected something was concealed in the fun of it. What was that black thing doing down there? Nobody noticed it, though it was as busy as the devil himself, turning a crank, keeping the show going. The people were gaping up at the showman, and did not see the strings being pulled. The strings gave his eloquent arms those noble flings, and opened and shut his mouth. That black thing at the back worked the oracle, but it had no face. It kept its head out of sight. The rest of it seemed to be a man, though it ought not to have been a man; but there is no chance in a crowd ever moving onward to stand to make sure of anything. That showman above was plain enough. He was a famous man. He was a man of the people. His portrait was often in the papers. One night he was in the study with Dad, and very merry. He was smiling tonight, as his mouth opened and shut, making hopeful sounds, keeping all going the right way for the good of everybody.

Stephen wanted to escape from the mob, but he was

in it. He was at home. He had to move with it to the next booth. That one belonged to a medicine man, by the look of him, and he was telling everybody of a cure-all for our troubles. He was young and serious, and wore a conical hat covered with the cabalistic signs of a magician with full honors, who knew what the mob could never know. That showman was too sure of himself to be bothered by the trickiness of the flares. He was his own light, and he was giving it out. You could see he was the best that judgment had come to since the last witch was burned. Soon the best heads, like his, would know enough to roll up the sky; then all could see what was behind it—knowledge had gone as high as that. What he had to tell the listening gapers below him flowed as easily as it ought to when the crowd has to believe what it cannot make head or tail of. Diagrams and pictures hung behind the magician, as convincing as Euclid and algebra mixed up together when most reasonable; and they proved, so the showman said, that the riddle of the earth and sky was unlocked. They had got it at last. His wand tapped this out on his pictures to myriad mouths, all open, and all dumb, while he explained the good to come of so grand a discovery.

It was quite simple, when you knew it, and as frightening as it was helpful. This last discovery lifted us up to the power that the gods once pretended they had, though they never had it. On the other hand, if a silly mistake was made when turning the key on it, if the right words to unlock the matter were spoken by the wrong man, then the wallop that knocked Lucifer out of glory was nothing to what would strike us, so the showman said, and winked. He knew. The frightful thing could happen because some liars and a few fools were still left about, and one of them could fiddle with the key while nobody was giving proper attention.

That clever showman was still talking when the key was turned the wrong way, though whether by a liar or an idiot there was no time to see. It came like the burst of a gun. The diagrams shot together and whirled as one furious Catherine wheel, and the earth sank. The foundations of it went, and nothing was left for the feet. The mob surged off in a torrent going faster and faster as the earth sloped lower and lower. He grabbed for a holding, but all holdings were loose. He was carried along in a flood of heads sweeping down a swift place to what was below. The heads rolled over the verge of a gulf, but he was held, he was lifted clear, still breathing, and looked on. He could see thousands of eyes passing him in a flood, all appealing to him, and then going over, and going out. Nothing could be done. It was too late.

The gulf plunged to the bottom of henceforth. Down there the people piled up, a jumble of heads and legs, and fell as still as the broken things not wanted any more in a rubbish chute. The earth stretched away beyond the dump to an awful distance into the dark, and it was the bare mud of a cold star left to rot, with skeleton trees, dead pools, abandoned guns, and the forms of what once were men strewn as many as all the hopes sunk in the last day.

He had to get out of it. He must get indoors and tell

them. They ought to hear. A little time might still be left, and they could be saved; but he couldn't move a hand, and he couldn't cry out. He tried, but he could not shout. He was fixed, staring at what life had come to. Presently a pinpoint of day pierced the dark, and met his eyes.

The tiny ray expanded. It enlarged to a sunny round. Through that oriel in his night he looked into another world, out of his reach. He could see into a room of a house he did not know, a primrose wall with the morning sun on it, and a corner of a picture showing. If all the picture were there it would tell him what he wanted to know. He waited for more, but the escape from where he was fixed ceased to grow any more. Was somebody in that room? Why didn't they show themselves? Oh, let someone tear wide open that circle of sunlight, and let him out!

Someone came, and her profile remained in the round of light. He knew her. That was the girl in blue and white he caught sight of the night before when all went bad. How did she get into this place? Why didn't she stretch out her hand to let him out? She was busy talking to somebody else he could not see, and as gaily as if all were well, when it was not. He wanted to tell her everything, but she did not look at him. He tried, but could not cry out. The round of light diminished to a point again, and then went out.

TWENTY-SIX

The corner that Stephen had seen of a morning world he could not enter did not include Lucy. There she was, as though on her daily visit, but not within the black frame of his sight's imprisonment. She was brooding over him, another victim of universal wrong; for under the weight of loss she found sleep but briefly, and last night again her thoughts were icy sharp all through the hours. She brooded over him with an idealist's lack of faith in harsh circumstance. Whatever Nurse Bridget might say out of kindness, Lucy could not believe a difference was there. His handsome pallor, to her, was of the last sacrifice, and her tears came.

Bridget was quick to cheerfulness. She guessed, if this went on, Miss Gale would be in as grave a plight as her brother, but Lucy remained inattentive, except in courtesy. That trace of a frown he had was put there by a reflection from the wall. How easy it is to be cheerful, when the dying is not your own brother!

Nell Tapscott stood apart, behind Lucy. She was jolly sure Mr. Stephen's eyelids had fluttered, and would have told them so, but what she had to say about it wasn't wanted in this place, with all the swells and the doctors about. It seemed to her that he frowned as if he wished they wouldn't do it while the two of them were talking about him, and it wasn't like him to be vexed. That nurse had a voice to draw pity out of a dry well as deep as some people she knew, but she wouldn't get round Miss Lucy, not in a month of Sundays. No fear. Nell had also the strange notion that she had seen on Bideford quay, even there, somebody of the same stamp as the man in the next bed to Mr. Stephen; and this, too, she kept to herself, while comforted by a pleasant fancy out of happier days than this.

The sailor in that bed was, for the moment, not concerned with his neighbor. He could see that young gentleman whenever he wanted to by turning his head. But he rarely had three pretty women grouped before him, and close, with leisure to judge their respective merits and please himself. Which one? Two of the ladies had not so much as noticed he was there, but the other, the charmer at the back, in a hat that dispersed wartime's gloom with roses, had smiled at him when their eyes met; and her color and abundance were to be preferred to delicate superiority. She was indulgent; she was all right.

"I assure you," said Nurse Bridget, "that he took us yesterday by surprise. Dr. Pickles had only just gone through the ward when he sat up—yes, he sat up, and quite strongly, and we thought he was going to speak. Perhaps it was as well he didn't, he looked so severe; and I don't believe he is forbidding, really, is he?"

Lucy did not say. He was white and still enough then.

She did not confess that she would love severity from him in a look, if he would give her so little. She could sleep on that. She thanked the nurse, and turned to go, and Nell followed. She left without another glance at Stephen, as his image would be with her all day, and until next morning. Nell, as she went, risked another smiling glance at the sailor, faint but favorable, out of a reminder of Bideford far away, and the peace and quiet of the hills of home. The sailor, surprised that this should come to him again, and satisfied, accepted it as his due. He felt better already as he watched the departure down the ward of a hat noticeably large, yet in its bold and sinuous grace appropriate to its wearer.

TWENTY-SEVEN

The two women passed the warden at the hospital gates on their way to a bus stop. He did not see them. The alert was on—it had been for the past hour, but now a delivery of hate was on its way direct, and the warden was intent on its apparition aloft, and so were all those who stood about. Lucy was not aware of their fixed attitude of expectancy. She did not see them. She was looking to the ground. Nell, at the increase of a growling roar, caught Lucy's arm firmly to check her, and turned to follow the common gaze.

There it came, fast as a huge black dart skimming the roofs. She judged its fall with the eye of one used to a boat's tiller while conning a swift approaching craft. She hauled Lucy over to the shelter of a flint wall, and added the protection of her body. She watched the threat shoot past overhead. Its end in a by-street was marked by an immediate ascent of dirty brown smoke, and then the blast swept them.

Lucy seemed to be barely aware of the incident, rousing sharply only to the burst and the smoke rising. Her servant retained a firm hold on her arm. O Lord, this lady was as silly as a two-year-old! Besides, she was more wilful than a little pig. She would not look after herself, not with the devil about, as he was all day long. Talk at her till you wanted to scream, she'd still go about like Widow Gollop—you know, after the poor soul saw one evening her old man's face staring at her out of the bedroom mirror. You can't do much with that, nobody could, and God help that fool Hitler if many of these Cockneys were like Miss Lucy.

From a bus window, Nell was alert for portents. At a time when anything may happen any minute, you want all the notice you can get. She watched the faces of the people on the pavement with concern, as faces are as good for warning as the clouds are when you wonder whether today means oilskins. You can't hear what is going on in the worrying rumble of a bus—you might be in the gutter any minute with the broken glass while wiping your nose. Besides, a bus is no better than a glass cupboard on the move in the open, not like a deep cellar. Her throat felt tight, too small for breathing. The day wasn't really cold, but she might be a shivery-shake. She was sure she couldn't put up with this nightmare, all wide awake, not much longer, not with the parapets everywhere ready to drop down on you and as many as the best apples in a westerly snorter, and no time to look up either. She couldn't go on smelling wet plaster and gas-escapes, it got up her nose, and no wonder she had lost weight.

The shop fronts along this route were a cruel sight, saying all the way the monsters were often there you never knew when. You had no more time than to flop flat on the stones and count five with your mouth on the curb while waiting to be done for. If you were counting when it blew up, you were still alive. Being hustled through life was a plague and not worth having, yes, and hustled out of it any minute as all the pickings you'd ever get for doing your best perhaps this very next minute.

They were getting on. All right so far. Here was the post office, eleven o'clock and only two panes of glass gone, and halfway now to the station. After that came wide open space in the train all the way to town and God come with us. . . .

What was that man staring at? Grinning and pointing up at something not to be seen through the roof of a bus? The bus stopped with a jolt, lurching them against the next seat. Nell jumped up to drag her mistress out of

127

it, but saw on the pavement beside the bus a woman with a shopping bag flat on her belly and terror in her face twisted round to see something that was falling on them.

No time to get out. Nell shut her eyes to count five and reached three when it burst ahead of them, and the baker's window alongside the bus shattered into a million pieces all over the woman on the pavement, and the poor thing flew into hysterics while the bus driver laughed back at the pale conductress as he started off again, and took a side-turning to dodge the smoke and dust.

Here was the station at last. Nell sighed. The face of the woman twisted up in horror from the pavement to the sky was still plain in her mind. "Nellie," said Miss Lucy, "you should have put on a warmer coat. Haven't you got one? You seem to be cold. The bright sun is deceptive."

Nell felt she must sob, but got over it, and soon began to watch the scenery go by on the journey to London. Where was Miss Lucy taking her to? She hadn't said. She never did speak till she had to. How the nesh little body could do this journey and back day after day and not wear out and no bones about it was more than could be known, except that suicide didn't matter. She was as hard as Lundy Island granite, and as pale, the mite. Never changed color whatever happened; she had no color to change. But it didn't suit the large and plump, who couldn't help her breasts shaking when doing no more than set the table when there was nothing worse to expect than the post.

This was restful. Her breathing was not so stop-and-start-again as it had been. Outside all was thankfully ordinary, so far, not like the wholesale smashing up of the blessed things you can't do without. Only empty roads and trees were asleep beyond the train window, and thank God for the calm of cows without a care. Why, she'd be getting drowsy watching hedges and telegraph poles going by like counting sheep. Indeed, she believed she did doze off for a minute, tired out doing nothing, for here they were running into Clapham Junction.

Not far to go now, but London had a name for catching it. There were tales about it you didn't want to believe, but had to. Well, Miss Lucy could put up with it and she would have to learn how to do it. She wished this day were over and done with. Though the nights were as bad and sometimes worse more often than not, and a deep cellar was the only comfort if cold . . . A rare lot of people on this platform, great crowds of them . . . Was London moving out? Why?

And mostly women. Women carrying infants and bundles, toddlers everywhere, no hats, straight you'd say from the kitchen and off in a hurry with their little lot, and if the saucepan's forgotten it can boil over if it wants to, no time to waste, and they were pressing up against the train before it stopped. In half a minute that compartment was jammed tight, no more standing room and the hatracks piled up. The mothers were gasping short and quick, though they kept cool while craning their heads about tallying the kids. Then they settled with a sigh.

A youthful mother apologized to Miss Lucy. "Excuse me, miss, was that your foot? Couldn't stand any more of it, not with a nipper tugging at me while the tiles were flying off. My place must look after itself tonight and I wish it luck."

In front of Nell, almost submerged in the press, was a slight figure with tousled gray hair and an aged face downcast, that had been deeply graved by fate. Her eyes were closed, in apparent submission to this last infliction, which mattered less than in former days, for surely it was the end of the punishment for whatever it was she had done.

"Has today been so bad?" asked Miss Lucy.

"Bad? You'd say so, lady," said another voice. "Any old underground station tonight for me. When I couldn't see for smoke how much of my street was left, I got the wind up."

The eyes of the old woman opened as she lifted her head, eyes shining through her wild hair as if she had wakened into youth. "Is it wind up?" she cried. "I declare to God it would blow the shirt tails through the neck band of the best man in the finest country that was made, and 'tis Donegal, and that I were there this minute."

Even Miss Lucy smiled. The soldier leaning over to grasp a hatrack for support was cuddling an infant, and the baby seemed convulsive with the soldier's silent laughter.

No more was said. There was not so much as a whim-
per from a child. Everybody might have been absorbed
in thought. The compartment waited in silence for Vic-
toria, and nobody moved, except to the swaying of the
train. The exodus at the terminus was deliberate and
quiet, but a boy's advice was shrill as he alighted.
"Mother, don't forget the rabbit on the hatrack."

TWENTY-EIGHT

Lucy looked round on the rivers of disheveled people
pouring down the platforms to converge and to be lost
in illimitable London as though here were no more than
a scene in the usual round of twenty-four hours; or, anyhow, a sight that should be expected in the unfolding of
history, and nothing for wonder. Nell responded to it
with a sense of urgency, which had to be firmly restrained, which wasn't easy. She must walk at the leisured pace of her mistress. She was not the one to hurry,
as a rule, nothing like it, but now she wanted to run,
though she didn't know which way to go.

They shuffled through glass by shattered shop fronts
outside the station. Lucy gave closer interest to the station approach, in which a wrecked bus stood in the

131

wrong place, disregarded and forlorn. "There was nothing wrong here yesterday," she explained to Nell.

"Ten minutes ago, miss," said a policeman standing by. "And this little lot isn't much of a sample of the day's work."

"Then they must be busier than they were."

"Is that it? All I know is the red light's been on all day, so far, and till it goes out I can't slip off for a cup of tea."

"Has any place of importance been hit?"

"Ah," said the policeman, "not unless you find it. If you don't find it you'll hear about it some day. Up to now, miss, they haven't got you and me."

Nell, who was glad of a small area of safety while standing, as she was, close to a large and calm policeman, noticed that Miss Lucy smiled once more. That was the second time in a day, so things must be looking up, despite appearances.

Lucy signed to a taxicab. "Waterloo," she ordered. "Get in, Nellie."

What is she up to now? wondered Nell. Surely she isn't going away right out of it? All the better if she is. Let it be as far as she can go, and soon. Nobody can get used to war, when it is on the door mat day and night, breakfast to supper, between meals and in bed with you. And Waterloo was a station she loved. That was where you could see a train going to Torrington. Or you used to be able to. There a train could be seen, with the good name on it, quite natural, ready to go there. Did a Torrington train still run? Well, she knew it did in dreams, and regular; and dreaming that you are where you are not is all that is left to quiet people in this frightening world. She was thankful the green light was up again. All clear! And so it ought to be, at Waterloo.

She recalled, following her mistress into the booking hall and waiting for what was to come, that after sleepy hours but no sleep in the night train, and a cup of tea at Salisbury if you are quick about it, you come to Barnstaple, and there it is morning. Soon after that the train rounds a corner by the tidal flats of the rivers where the dunlin flies upwheeling like a little cloud of smoke, and the sea opens out. The western sea is there, and the white stalk of Braunton lighthouse stands, just as ever, over its yellow sandhills; and across the water, as calm as the sky, the white houses of Appledore wind round the foot of its green hill and are looking straight at you as if they knew you were on your way. . . .

Miss Lucy was speaking to her, and Nell was startled back into the present moment and common sense.

"Now, Nellie, here you are. You can get all you need." She handed Nell a purse and a ticket. "Take care of that ticket. You see what it is, don't you? Now put it in your purse. There you are. The Torrington train leaves in twenty minutes. Go home."

Nell's chin dropped. "Oh, Miss Lucy, m'dear, don't you want me?"

"Yes, but I mustn't keep you. I hope to see you again as soon as this is over. Write to me, please. I remember how good you were to my mother. But to stay here is unpleasant."

"Aren't you coming too?"

"No. I cannot leave London."

"Then I'm not going. I won't go. I'll stay where you are. I don't care."

Lucy frowned. She was perplexed. She was irresolute. Her maid was holding that purse awkwardly, as if there was nowhere to put an unwanted gift; and by that token she understood there is something in another person above logic, and beyond speech. It came to her mind that she had once known distaste for this girl, and now she was embarrassed. It began to be clear that reasoning on facts is powerless when memory and affection are opposed. Now what could she say?

"Don't send me away."

Her mistress made no sign, except to raise her arm sharply to glance at her watch, which Nell took to mean that time was being wasted, and there wasn't much of it left.

"Then," said Lucy, "I can't help you if you won't let me. You must stay here, if you won't go home, though I really thought the noises were worrying you. . . . Very well. We'd better find another taxi. Come along. I'm already very late."

"Miss Lucy, wait a minute." She touched Lucy's arm. "This ticket. Please. Don't you think you'd better get your money back?"

Her mistress laughed, and Nell opened her eyes to hear it. She had never heard Miss Lucy laugh before, and it was such a light one, and came easy to her. She must have done it before, in the days when fright was not in every street all day long, for it to rise in her as quick as the sun comes out of a cloud.

They were leaving the station, when above the multiple distractions of the traffic there sounded a more compelling note. That dreary wailing again! The red light was showing. And only the heart of honesty would laugh now, thought Nell, with the warning howling again right into the bowels. It would shake the inside of a saint, to say nothing of a proper old trembler like herself.

TWENTY-NINE

A destroyer, with Sir Anthony Gale aboard, and below, was heading across the Channel for Portland. It was foul weather. She belied her part in human affairs. She had not the likeness of a destroyer. Out there she had no apparent significance at all. She was but showing valiancy in keeping her speed this side of being expunged by elemental powers in unrest.

At half a mile, she would have been made out by an observer with difficulty. She was all but lost in the drive of a blustering westerly, under somber clouds that were down to the waves at the limit of sight. She became plain only when a rift torn in the gray ceiling released a shaft of the sun, a brief illumination that sped like the withdrawal of hope athwart the dun waste. When that beam met her, there she was, a black object for a moment, her funnels wildly rocking amid breakers brilliant as snow. The beam gone, then valiancy was invisible in shadow, and a looker-on out there, himself beset, might speculate about her, if he had the leisure and interest to do it.

Sir Anthony, thrown about below in the little ship, made up his mind, if slowly and prudently. He would face it in the open. It couldn't be much worse up above.

He rubbed a bruised arm. This painfully small room had too many unexpected corners. They must be nearly across by now. He had had all he could enjoy of a short voyage from a Normandy beachhead. How these giddy young bucks with him put up with this sort of thing, and joked about it—part of their day's work—was a puzzle he still had to think out. He didn't understand them. He had even begun to wonder what would happen to such as himself if these spry happy-go-luckies were not willing to suffer this sort of life, while waiting for the summons to attend to crises. At the same time, he had noticed there was not one among the amusing cards he had spoken to aboard who was worth more than shillings, as an aid to a wise directive intelligence intent on real work with a satisfactory per cent margin of profit.

The queer thing was that he was nothing among them; or not more than a dummy standing in the way of their hurried passage. He was aware that he chilled the exchanges of their family jokes. He didn't believe they had ever heard his name before, though they misled him politely about that while advising him how not to get himself damaged, as long as he was in their care. They would suffer for it, if he got hurt. They deferred, as well as he could make out, to nobody but a mysterious outside authority, unseen by them, and unknown to him, yet familiar to everyone aboard as Mickey.

Her behavior, they explained to him—they always spoke of their ship as a woman they had known all their lives—was a wanton, and that wasn't their fault. So she was born. But once you were on good terms with her you knew what to expect, and occasionally got it. She didn't care a hoot for the First Lord himself, should his holy feet stand on her deck, to say nothing of dukes, and they had had that well rubbed in. And didn't they know it! She was as bad as the worst you could call her when she had made up her mind to let them have it.

Mickey, who ordered them out of the invisible what to do with her, and changed his mind about it whenever the mood took him, and who used them, to tell the truth, as the slaves of his bloody lamp, never realized what she was able to do, no, nor what she would flatly refuse to do though she had always done it before. He, Sir Anthony, no doubt supposed she was an abandoned girl, yet in fact she was a beauty, and they wouldn't exchange her for a noble battleship. He could tell that to the Admiralty, as well as to the marines.

The wild and difficult way of making a living these men preferred, Sir Anthony surmised, while standing alone, holding tight to a stanchion, must have been going on in the world for quite a long time. It appeared to be natural to them; though he himself had only known it hitherto as an abstraction called Tonnage. The loss of tonnage, officially, was a grave matter. That was about all he knew. Still, and he must freely admit it, these men could turn their complicated box of tricks into a bird as free as the wind, and without perceived trickery, when unexpectedly an enemy plane—it was near and coming fast before he knew it—dived on them out of the clouds to drop its bombs—which he himself saw falling —and they nearly deafened him without warning with their blasting derision of the foe.

As if nothing much had happened, they turned about and sped for home, pretending they knew where it was in a blind confusion of dark weather and uproar. Now they had just announced that he would be ashore ahead of the clock. He hoped so. There before him was what they called home, though he saw it as only another dark-ish smear of misery, to change for the worse at the next howl of the wind.

As he went ashore he was accorded a formal salute, but had the fancy that their courtesy was not without a touch of jovial mockery. He was grateful for this solid concrete under his feet again, and never mind the rain. Was it solid? His faith was always in reinforced concrete, and yet walking on it here had a disconcerting difficulty. Was nothing to be trusted? He was unable to stride away from the warship with dignity, and those sailors were watching him. The quay behaved in an indecently drunken manner, heaving heavily up and down under him in memory of a deck. Quite a few of his other fixed ideas, too, were working loose.

THIRTY

He settled himself with more assurance into the kind of car that is reserved for important personages, and his right self began to return to him. He hoped Lucy would be at Budmouth to meet him. There should be news, either good or nothing worse. And a report had to be drafted. He would sooner do that quietly here than in London, where other problems would be poured over him to bury this latest mission, and what he thought of it. He began to breathe again in ease and comfort.

One thing he knew. One thing for certain. If another visit to the battle front became necessary, let a deputy do it. Once was enough. Never again for him. Let another clever person go over to get his notions unstuck, and find a new set, if he could. Orderly notions over there are blown up and get jumbled into a welter, like the shell holes and mine craters. What wise advice could any man offer on the horrific, when horror is a daily necessity? It would be just the same if he were as sound as Solomon; he'd never get it straight. No more of it for him.

He might have known it; perhaps he ought to have known it. Something he remembered. There used to be Nicholas on this subject of combat, once on a time, cynical and funny, and too often. He recalled that burly and good-natured man with less discomfort than in a time past. There was, he thought now, some truth in Nick's wicked drollery. He was too busy at the time to give it thought. He had no room for it in his head. A day came, and sooner than was expected, when we were fighting for our existence; there was no doubt about that. None whatever. Desperation was forced on us. What time had we then for thought, except how best to keep our vitals intact?

What else was there to think about? Yet it now began to appear that a battlefield, a quite unavoidable and righteous battlefield, had not the clean stamp of a chessboard. It was nothing like the noble game played by thinkers at a board they can't see—because it is oceans and continents—moving about on it invisible items of power to surprise unseen opposites with weightier chessmen. It looks like that at the center, where the moves are ordered; but there are consequences, and now he had seen them in the incidental and unpredictable balks and impediments on the ground itself, where the flames are; and these had to be paid for. There were too many of them. They add up the wrong way. They damp the cheering. They confuse a statesman's high intelligence when he follows up the guns to see what they have done. His own tour of inspection had provided too much detail.

It could be said that in this last experience of his, where the machine guns were at work, there was one benefit; and he was very glad of the least good thing in it. From today he ought to be far better at advice. . . . Yes? Better? He would be?

Yet suppose, in this bedevilment of the earth, the better idea turns out to have the worst hidden in it? When the right move to make, by all that a good conscience knows, has hidden in it most of the pains of hell, then common sense itself isn't what it was. And where to find a substitute for common sense?

His thoughts went back to Bewley, where a home used to stand. He had supposed horror was in personal disaster. He had reason. Anybody else would have thought so; but no, it is not, not quite. Dismay isn't horror. Dismay is instant. Horror comes over you slowly, you don't know how. It isn't seen coming. The look of things changes, and when it has blackened sunlight you can't tell anybody. Nobody sees it but you, and the old meaning goes out of life. He had had his lesson. How pass it on?

What a world, in which men will see, round about some midnight, bewitched by the twelve strokes of it, that life would be better as carrion! War! We change round life and death. Give death the first place. Bash in the lively faces. Burn out laughter. Find the artful way to mangle and blind whole populations. To the pit with the lot. Death improves us. The mistake about life is that it was ever made. Turn it into muck. Give it to the festering flies. He had failed to notice that when at the council table, with only good resolutions and white blotting paper before him.

What was the matter with him? Those faces he had seen lying about, with flies hovering about them, that he couldn't forget, they were nothing to him, were they?

He paused when within the hotel to collect himself. He was wandering. His wits had loosened. "Has Miss Gale called for me?"

"No, sir."

He went slowly upstairs. Old. Getting old, that was it. Or going ga-ga. Both.

While steadying himself on the landing he was greeted by a colleague. "Glad to see you safely back, Sir Anthony. You must have had a beastly crossing, I'm afraid. It goes very well over there, does it not?"

"Quite well. Nearing downfall, I thought. They'll soon be on the run."

"Almost Te Deum time?"

"That's it."

THIRTY-ONE

He would wait for Lucy. He settled himself in his room. He would not move, he would see nobody, till he had seen her. That girl was pretty good at the nature of things; and, if she remained silent, which was her way, still she was aware. As he saw her, she was all that was left that he could believe in, now. And Stephen. How was the boy?

Sir Anthony looked with concern at the clock again. Too soon. Nearly an hour to go before the next train was in. He would rest until she came. A space of silence by himself would help.

The demands and obsessions he had experienced at sacred Headquarters could bide a wee. Fervid ideas and hot antipathies muddled together while people perished in multitudes had given him a sense of urgency as useful as incoherence. What wisdom he had formed of it must stand till it was clear of foreign matter. If anybody wanted the truth of it, let them ask the archangel Michael; perhaps he knew. As for himself, he was mortal, and he was tired.

Where was Lucy? Why wasn't she there? What he wanted was that girl's steady heart and light touch. She would give him quiet.

If only the doubts whirling over France would stand for a minute they could be seen for what they are. But volcanic eruptions don't settle down till the worst is done. The truth is hidden beneath a pall of smoke with blood running out from under it.

Nothing keeps quiet over there but the faces without names. Anonymous faces, often disfigured, identity lost. That officer, propped up by a cottage door, with a smile imprinted on his yellow wax as if at a permanent joke. Whoever looked at him suspected living men were the joke. What is dead and done for—left where it drops as the uproar and smoke progresses, no good to anybody any more—that only is patient, and makes no impossible demands.

Yet what concern had those figures scattered all over the landscape with him? None. They weren't his business over there. Nothing like it. He didn't know them. You come across them, and there they are. They don't see you. You see them. They have come to an end, but won't be gone. Faces. Like Stephen's face. All young, and all dead. Was that train in yet? . . . Damn that telephone.

Perhaps it was Lucy at last. He lumbered up and over to the unrelenting instrument, but was disappointed. "Yes, speaking. Who? Oh, how d'ye do. Thank you, I'm very well. What's that? . . . I've only just got in. . . . You wish I would? Then I suppose you'd better come up."

A bore, of course, and not what he was waiting for. Here it began, as ever. And he suspected he had in himself today the drab intelligence a bore ought to know is his, but never does.

What he really wanted was a little sleep. The shadow of it was coming over his eyes. It was due to him. Instead, an important body was on his way upstairs to talk. Whenever refuge in peace and quiet was yearned for, to restore his balance, then it always happened that someone was knocking at his door to settle a question, which did no more than raise ten more. Never a pause.

144

Would there ever be escape from what others think you ought to do?

He hoped, anyhow, he would appear to be properly attentive while this interview lasted. "Come in, sir, come in! How is it with you, General? Sit down—throw those papers on the floor."

"I won't keep you, Sir Anthony. I'll be away in a few minutes. You'll be weary. I've seen the unfriendly weather reports. I expect, like me, you loathe the sea. It's an unnatural place for a soldier."

"Yes, but there it is. The story goes that there it was before we went on it. One may still learn something while afloat."

The soldier smiled. "We've been learning it—how to scramble clear of it just before being drowned."

Sir Anthony closed his eyes, as if to consider this. The air was languorous. He must fight this sleepiness. Learning! He could see, with his eyes shut, his destroyer backing away in the shallows over there. A glassy wave swelled up under his nose, and a boy's head rolled round in it, stared up at him dimly through the glass, open-mouthed, and then rolled over.

A voice was droning on. It wasn't that boy's voice. No water was in it. It was quite distinct, but far. It would be an honor if he would. His staff would be glad . . . before you return to London, Sir Anthony.

Sir Anthony roused himself. He opened his eyes to find this voice. He had just saved himself from dropping right off.

"You were saying?" he asked.

His visitor felt sorry for Sir Anthony. He had been overdoing it. He was too old for tanks in action and frights. "Nothing, sir. But we're in your debt here. My people are hoping you will visit them before you return to town. We've been surprised when material we badly wanted, and had no hope of getting, came along not too late. You've had your eye on us. Do come and hear us say it, won't you?"

Sir Anthony appeared to be solemnly thinking this over. His patient visitor thought he need not be so long and solemn about so small a thing.

The old boy certainly did look pale and weary. And, since at last there he was, that head before him was good enough for a soldier's. It looked the part. He thought he had seen something like it in a picture of an old Mongol conqueror. His mouth told everybody that the feelings of others never worried him, or not much. He had his own way. All the same, he hadn't yet said what he would do about this. Had he gone to sleep?

The door opened abruptly, and a lady entered, swiftly and brightly. The soldier rose. He saw who this young woman must be. There was no mistaking such an elegant little reminder of the important person in the chair. She gave him a glance sharp with authority, and went straight to the reclining figure.

"I think he has this very moment fallen asleep," explained the soldier.

Lucy bent to her father indulgently, and kissed his forehead. He did not respond. She recoiled, and still he made no sign. She stood over him in wide-eyed shock,

146

then fell to her knees by his chair and seized a limp and yellowing hand. "Daddy," she cried.

There was no answer. There was no movement in the room till she turned her face up to the officer standing over her. "He's gone," she said, "he's gone."

Her voice sounded like treachery to memory, and she remained on her knees, staring at her father, fixed by his mask. Then her head fell on her father's shoulder. Her hat tumbled off as if the truth had struck panic into it. It began to roll away over the floor in flight, but weakly collapsed.

THIRTY-TWO

In holiday weather, the beach at Budmouth is a shining crescent of sand and shingle recessed between two dark uplands that stand well out into the unrest of the sea. Those heights that embay the beach seem always, whatever the cheer of the moment, to be of another age than this, remote and grave; as grave as if the rocks out there were as far off as antiquity itself. And in fact they do bear advice, for whoever cares to spell out their inscribed hieroglyphics, that a strange life was busy and abundant hereabouts eons before man was so much as foreshadowed on earth. But the beach itself remains innocent of

147

the impress of the past, and reflects, especially to children, only the glad sunshine of the hour. It was here—or so the story goes, and Fanny Burney had a woman's eye for what she was looking at—that George III used to dip in the tide, while a loyal band struck up "God Save the King" whenever the anointed head disappeared under water.

There is a promenade above the beach, and along it the young naval commander—who had, within the hour, safely landed Sir Anthony Gale—was striding purposefully on his way to report to headquarters. The beach below him had hardly any interest and purport for him. The weather was clearing. He noticed that. Time it did, with the work in hand. Old Gale didn't enjoy that last run. What a grim old bird! The officer knew he wouldn't care to exchange business signals with that mouth and nose. It was good for these high-ups, once in a while, to get the full flavor of salt water with gun smoke. Then they knew more than before.

The sailor was barely aware of the people strolling about, except that there were too many of them. These idlers were in the way; though it did occur to him that the war was getting on quite nicely for everybody since girls were out and about again in abbreviations and towels, sunning themselves. He had forgotten that attraction used to exist, and it was a promise of ease for the future which softened, in a casual glance, the immediate unrelenting compulsion of cramped quarters, full knots in hard weather, and explosions.

He did halt once to scan the horizon. The smoke of a

convoy of barely visible ships was rising above the sky-line, coiling over a clear belt of greenish sky. That was a noble spread of dead weight for France. And the wind had shifted. Perhaps it would be easier for that lot. For his part, if seas could be expected pretty often through his term to be as ugly for small craft as the Channel in a disobliging mood, then give him a stick and the navigation of cows.

The sea was ebbing from the shallow beach. A wide area of wet sand was exposed, so responsive to the sun, when it showed itself, that the distinction between land and water was lost in glare. From that luminous space seaward the cries of children blew landward as sharp and small as the piping of birds; music satisfying and as old as the hills to man, when looking round at leisure on his world, yet barely noticed. What was remarkable on that beach, down towards the water, was a high bar-rier, a lattice of steel scaffolding stretching for miles be-tween the promenade and the line of low tide. That bar-rier had been erected on the sands in the anxious weeks not long since to check the enemy, when he invaded England, for he was expected shortly to arrive, if weather and affairs favored him. The steel lattice was to be aided by gunfire from posts hidden on the overlook-ing hills.

That day, when the young commander was nearing his headquarters, the gun emplacements secreted on the slopes of the amphitheatre made providential shelter for lovers, and the barrier seaward, meant to hinder the advance of the monsters of battle, was affording amusement to children at their gymnastic larks. They were climbing about the lattice then, moving distantly as monkeys in the bare spars of a geometrical forest standing in the fabulous.

The naval officer accepted this change in the order of nature as appropriate as is a gun platform or the call to dinner, though he had to peer through the steel forest for the horizon. Like everybody else there that day, free in an interval of holiday to observe at ease the appearance of things, he accepted the more recent local additions of grotesquerie to the proofs of human dominance as no more to be questioned than grass.

He crossed the road to his headquarters. On the steps of those offices, once a fashionable hotel, he stood aside to allow a group of people to descend. A stretcher was in their midst. He was used to stretchers, but this one was out of place. Only a pair of boots was exposed on it, and he doubted them, though they betokened high caste. They were not under control. He had learned long before that much is given away by the manner the feet are disposed, when only feet are showing on a stretcher. Had one of the high hats dropped off?

The stretcher was followed by a woman so lost in thought that, coming out of the shade into the dazzle, she stumbled at the first step. She might have fallen had not the ready hand of the sailor restored her balance.

Lucy met his eyes. She saw the rigor melt on the officer's upturned face, that fixity of purpose which vigilance and restraint fashion in the expression of a dutiful man. She would have thought him a severe officer but for that swift change to good nature.

His impulse was not altogether from dutifulness. His instant smile was more as if in that moment he was fortunate. What a bright and sharp little person! But too pale. She needed care, and his luck had landed him there in the right minute to give a little. He was also sure that he would prefer not to be in the way of those light eyes, their long black lashes directing their scrutiny, if the occasion were other than sociable.

Lucy, recovering her poise, held his regard, which was firm, for a second or two longer than the obligation required. He pleased her. She saw in him the same casual strength and charity that she had remembered too late of Stephen, when gentle with a mental crisis.

She lowered her eyes, and passed. The commander turned to watch her descend. No weakness was there. It was perfect assurance. Had she any interest in that stretcher? No. No sign of it. The ambulance turned one way, and she another.

She turned towards the town, and he watched her long enough to surmise that she was addressed to some business in a hurry. He could see she was unaffected by a day freed from the menace that had long held that shore in thrall. She was not holiday-making. Her slight figure, slipping along swiftly, was lost almost at once in the flow of leisurely traffic. It would not occur to him that she was but trying to walk away from her shadow, which could only be done with a quick step.

Lucy became aware of the contented people about her

when the footpath narrowed, and she was brought to a stand. Idle faces imprisoned her. She was separated from her reverie, and was kept from catching up with it. Despair came over her, and she sighed. That the drive of her thoughts was only for herself, and that nobody else felt it, came with the shock of the discovery that the labored soul, in the stir of mankind, is alone.

A crowd of women about the shops, with market baskets and children, gazing at what she could not see and had no wish to see, were as indifferent to her need, and to all else, as if when they paused then the hour stood still for everybody. She was beset. Her first impatience with this ignorance about her surged into desperation. It was an alien and a cruel world. How could it be suffered? She could not go on like this. She would have to break with it.

When a space began to clear for her escape, and she moved to take it, a child's carriage was at her feet. It had been submerged and unseen. Lucy made brusquely to push it clear, but was stayed by the gaze of the child in it. The infant was lost in placid consideration of what was in the sky above, seen only by itself. Innocence was in its own world, and was as lonely as she was.

Their eyes met. In instant communion the child beamed on her, as if trust in its own kind is always right. The child offered for sharing a gnawed apple, as a sign.

Lucy bent to touch the face of innocence, and was unprepared for its springy tenderness. The slight contact quieted her. How odd, that such fragility, mortal as a rose petal, was expected to meet the blind trampling she knew, and yet keep to the last the color of its beginning! The poor little mite!

An unseen hand broke the secret communion. Released from the traffic, Lucy found a side-turning, and welcomed it. Its emptiness promised that it led to nothing popular. It brought her to a broad strand at the back of the houses. It was a sort of limbo for boats, yachts, and ships' gear, not wanted for these present years, of no use in war. Those acres of gravel were oblivion for things that once gave lightness of heart. A fleet of small yachts was hauled up before her, high and dry, out of sight of their flowing element.

The little ships were weather-stained and neglected. They had been taken out of life, shored-up, and abandoned when ill befell everybody with gunfire. Except an old man and a dog, she had the place to herself. She was drawn over to what so accorded with her own desire to be out of it all.

She could believe she knew that one. It had been a yawl. She stood beneath the bulge of it, its form as sharp and compact as a kittiwake's. It was blistered and peeling. It was much the same as Stephen's *Gipsy*. And what had become of his little cruiser? She had, till that moment, lost sight of it. It was half buried in the silt of an Essex creek, of course, where it had been left. It was years since this one, too, was lively and free.

She laid a hand on its body. It was warm in the sun, as if heat were still in it, and it might rouse to movement again, if called.

Would there be another call to life? Was that possible, when so little that mattered remained in the heart? How could fair morning rise again out of the silt of the years?

No. It could not. No such sunrise as she had seen, after rubbing sleep from her eyes, from the *Gipsy's* deck. Nothing so good as that ever again. There Stephen was, when she was up on deck, a little shivery in the cold newness of day, there he was with his pipe—she smelt his pipe before she saw him—squatting by the mainmast, lost in contemplation. A family of mallard was alongside, muttering quite friendly. There was no other sound. The tide was beginning to rise into that Essex creek. The samphire on the tidal mud was smouldering crimson, nearly in flames, and the mud was polished silver. Autumn in the marshes, where there is nothing in sight but the complete round of the sky, and nothing much under the sky but yellowing rushes and the black ruin of a fisherman's hut, and a long way off another mast prominent as the only sign that you are not in the center of isolation—it all told her then, but she didn't know it, that a particular quiet moment will still mean something when the tumultuous occasions have gone and have left no meaning. For Stephen, just looking on as usual, was as much at his ease as the ducks. He refused to take that tide and go. "It's all right here," he grumbled. "Why bother to find a worse thing?"

Yet they left it. She saw to that. They went. She never had much patience. Not long after they met a southeaster, and very likely would have finished up on the Gunfleet Sands but for his strength and his sympathy with his ship. The ship seemed to know better than she did why he wanted one way and not another.

Ah, if only it were possible to rest in the past, to stay there, like the *Gipsy*, a ghost with other ghosts, out of reach of change and chance! If only she could get back now into a Budmouth that was, out of this busy one, for she remembered there was an old bridge in it. That nice old bridge must have gone by now. It wasn't likely she could find it, for it was no more than one of the earliest pictures in her mind, and almost as far back as she could see. Father stood by her that evening. He was talking quietly to someone—and who was it?—he was talking almost in a whisper, as if what was there in the twilight might overhear him. Black water was below them.

She wandered on, with no sense of direction, and came to a bridge spanning a neck of water. Could this be it? The parapet she remembered was higher than this, but those buildings, dark and worn, rising out of the water, they were the same. The bridge itself was a new bridge of life, with nobody stopping to look over its parapet. Life today was men in all varieties of martial uniforms, and they passed over it endlessly, girls with them, girls hanging on to a last chance before battle.

Lucy paused and looked down on the harbor below. Strange. This must be the place of a time that had gone. Who was it Father was talking to here so earnestly long ago? They both spoke in undertones, but not to her. She was fascinated by those rugged buildings rising out of the water like sooty cliffs; and there they were now. She had thought they were as severe as grisly towers in a fairy tale, especially while that murmuring was going on beside her. Those severe warehouses at twilight would keep voices down to a whisper. The water that evening was deep under crowding shadows. Only odd reflections told her it was waiting down there.

Waiting for what? She was half frightened. Ships she could hardly see were asleep under the walls. Night was down below, but light was in the sky. Over the inky jags of the roofs was the moon. She had wondered why it was plain in the sky, when it was so thin that she thought she could see through it. The voices murmuring on, and the ghost of a moon above the chasm in which ships were in darkness, made her feel sad. Voices were in undertones, as if something was there, and everybody ought to know the worst, yet it must never be mentioned aloud, not for a child to hear.

Perhaps the prophetic vision of its brooding long ago, when she was very young, was this that she was looking at. The shape of things to come had met her. Now it could be seen. War. The breaking of homes. Yet everybody took it as ordinary, quite what you might expect, just as natural as children are to mothers.

She could not go on living with it. She knew she could not. To accept things as they are takes the meaning out of life. That peremptory shouting she could hear on the ships below was not in her world. Nor were those ships. Her ships were not there, those that slept in a twilight. They had gone, except from within the twilight of her memory. It was the full glare of another day, and new ships had come with it. There they were, reptilian monsters of steel, a full arrogant brood of them with ugly snouts. They crowded the harbor. They were fulfilment. She had lived long enough to see fulfilment.

Dreadful! Promise had gone from the earth, except the promise of worse things. Hope had gone. This was left, the ugly and deadly. Evil was left. She hated it. And what, she asked herself, can I do? What can I do?

Her arm was touched by a policeman. "I'd move on, miss, if I were you. Don't stand here. They're putting out a little fire in the ship under us, and she might, you know . . . she might go up. It's all right, so they say, but don't you wait."

THIRTY-THREE

Old Martin of Seven Stones, the farm tucked within a wooded hollow of High Down—you see it from the shore as a darkish oval patch high up and far away on the pale upland just under the skyline—was out seeking a lost beast. He had plenty of room in which to look for her; she might be anywhere, and she filled the eye of his master, who thought what a beauty she was. Martin would say for her she was a right good milker, when she was sociable, a nice little red beast of a Devon, and easy

157

to manage, if you knew how to do it, but not if you didn't, and not always when you did.

He had been out for her the evening before, but fog began to make on the high ground the way it does with a change of wind. He rambled to and fro among the areas of furze and bracken down to the lower slopes, and as far down as the thickets of blackthorn and bramble, and a scourge they are. Springs soak the ground there, black and sticky, and that was the hiding place to perish in, he guessed, as you'd still be there on resurrection day, all expense saved, and no fuss. The fog began to drift and weave about there too, so he straightened his back as well as he could, though he'd never get the warp out of it, and looked to the waters of the Channel, but saw nothing.

Better get back. All was blind. He might as well look for a lost pipe dropped somewhere about, and if it was the sweetest of his draws, let it go. She was a touchy creature, that lost one. She'd take huff, and off and away from the others, and was so neat a figure she must be pure blood, he judged, she was that girlish in her ways. And now, if she got tangled up in a thicket like this, she'd panic, very likely, and make a regular do of it, lose heart and die, the silly thing, when there was no call for it. She must put up with what she had asked for. After a day's work, he hadn't a lot of patience left over for the tricks of skittish high blood when there was the same grass for all.

Martin was out early next day. The fog had gone, but distinction had not come. There was a thinning of night.

Things in sight were deceptive. A stunted hawthorn by itself leaning awry on the seaward slope was humped much the same as a beast asleep. Anyhow, he was up betimes, so there was no hurry. All the same, there was the herd to see to whether she was found or gone. If the figure of her would only show up obligingly in front of him, as a surprise, he'd ask for no greater fortune. It would fill a hole in his thoughts. There's no sense in it, to be sure, but you'll get so used to another thing of earth that it becomes part of you, though you don't know it, except now and then as a worry; then one day it's gone, and there's left a draughty gap in your make-up past patching.

And now which road should he go, up or down or over the other side of the hill? She could be here or there, if anywhere at all. He'd own up to it there was something in prayer, if a man could expect heaven to bend an ear to this forgotten place about a lost cow, when rank and quality in a great war by sea and land were sending up cries for high judgment all day and all night. He could only leave it to what he knew of creatures; and that, he was sorry, was only what the beasts themselves knew, and they never tell.

While Martin was working his way through a coppice, and peering about within it, a secretive place that topped a rocky escarpment, the great void below became the sea. The specters that had loomed on the steep descent to the shore turned into plain bushes queerly molded by the winds. Martin broke through the dank and dim tangle of the little wood to meet sunrise. Like the burst of a silent explosion, day rayed through the lower bars of cloud, fired them, and established the earth.

He stood to take it in. Drying weather, most likely! He himself, in his working clothes, touched by gold, though unaware of it, was elevated there, briefly, as an image of man in his early dignity, looking round on his unblemished heritage.

Martin heard a rustling in the wood he had just left, and turned. The lost beast was following him. She ambled on and stood a little behind him, lifted her head, bellowed, then waited patiently on his next move.

"So there you are, Bess, are you! You've found me instead. It's all one." He looked her over. "We'll make for home. The best thing to do is to skirt this pitfall and take the path up from below. It's your easiest way. Come on, and no half-larks. I've had enough of you."

Man and beast went around the escarpment to a track under it. Martin stayed for a glance up at the overhanging rocks. He was seldom that way; nor was anyone else. It was a lonesome place. The horizontal early light favored the whitish cliff with a moonlike glow apparently its own, an illusion that gave wall, shelf, and buttress of horizontally stratified limestone a significance beyond chance sculpturing by wind and weather. It was more like ancient masonry downfallen, a stately house given up in a time out of memory by a family whose name was lost. A great bird floated away from an upper ledge and circled leisurely skyward.

"That's what I thought," Martin said to his beast.

"That's where those buzzards bide out of sight. We'll say nothing about it, in case."

His gaze roved down to the sward under the rocks, and steadied. What was that? It didn't belong here, that queer thing over there. What was it?

He went forward to where it sprawled partly within a recess in the base of the rocks, and his beast followed him. The heap began to stir, while Martin was still puzzling over its nature. Then it struggled to uprightness, and he stopped. A woman made uncertainly towards him.

She was young, and of the quality, but her dress could have been out of a hedge. Her hat and hair, too.

She spoke, and her voice and manner told him that his interest, which was in his stare, was not sought. She but wanted to ask a question. He could scarcely hear her. He bent his head to her thin voice.

"A fog came. I don't know where I am," she explained.

"You been there all night, miss?"

"I suppose so. There was a noise. A roaring a minute ago. It woke me. I don't know where I am. What is this place?"

"It's hard to say, miss." Martin's experience did not tell him how to address an apparition. Such a slip of a woman in that outlandish corner all night! She was as stray as a wet feather.

"You haven't answered me," she said sharply.

The fixity of purpose in her white face awed him. People lost their heads, he had heard, when wandering and sick.

"I think," said Martin, "first thing is, you better come along home with me. Don't you?"

"No," said Lucy. "I don't."

"I do, miss. It'd be right and tidy."

She did not answer.

"Can you walk, miss?"

"Of course I can." But Lucy was already aware that she had been on her feet too long. "I'll try," she added, courage becoming a little faint, and not quite sure of recovery.

"This is a rough pitch to try on, miss," Martin pointed out, "when you don't feel up to it. D'ye see, it's all easy, you do what I say. I've a great name hereabouts for hoisting a load. So you take hold of me. Eh? Yes, I say. Yes. Your arms round the neck. Now that's sensible. Lord, miss, you're as dewy as grass. No, not like that. This way. It'd be easier for me. That's right. That's the ticket. All right now? Then we're set. It's about time you were there. Not far to go, but home is up along."

THIRTY-FOUR

Lucy surrendered to what must be. She closed her eyes, as sight was no defense against the casual cruelty of an indifferent universe. Her defiance in adversity collapsed to simple trust in good-natured strength that supported freely, without question, and without effort, like an oak. All she knew of the journey up along to nowhere in particular was of warm puffs of a mingled smell of byre, sweat, and tobacco. It made her drowsy. She did not like the smell, and she did not dislike it. It was there. She could not be sure that sleep did not overcome her. She did not remember coming to a house.

She was in bed, when next she opened her eyes. An elderly woman was bent over her, with stony eyes and a critical frown, as in cold annoyance. Lucy made to rise, and checked a cry of alarm. The face near to her own was large, red and bony, and gray hair fluffed out about it like the untidy portents of storm.

"You be still. Rest 'ee," said the woman, and left her, going sideways through a door that was either very narrow, or else the woman was unusually wide.

Lucy was impelled to get up hastily, to escape, but saw at once in a small room, almost bare, that she must stay where she was. Her clothes were not there.

She sank back again into submission. What did it matter? A party of sparrows was arguing vivaciously on the window sill. A cock crew. Somebody in the house was moving about below. She could hear only those inconsequential sounds, never noticed except in a spacious silence, and by one who must remain alone and still, and listen for what news might come of the passing of time in a strange country.

The ceiling of the bedroom seemed to have had crammed into it the spare corners left over after the house was finished, but before the roof went on, when builders of homes had reasons we don't know for doing what they did. Except in a weird old German woodcut that Stephen found and hung up for his amusement, she had never seen anything like it. The black beam overhead held up a crazy medley of angles and arches.

Lucy noticed that it suited the spiders. Spiders used to make her shudder, for no reason at all, but she didn't object to them now, at a distance. She didn't feel able, at the moment, to object to anything. At least the spiders assured her that this place wasn't subject to disturbance.

It was a comforting thought, a place exempt from upsets. In the beginning she had faith, a little of it. Mother gave it to her. But Mother had knowledge of the unseen that, she doubted, would never come to her. If Paradise wasn't there, somewhere, then it ought to be, for Mother was a saint. Her own trifle of faith had grown less and less. All gone now. It isn't possible, is it, to watch what is going on in the world without dreading that all has gone too far already?

Her own dread did not begin with the war. She always knew the war was as sure to come as midnight to strike. Faith goes when the truth seems to be that God has left us to make what we like of cruelty and lies. She had hoped the war would come. Hoped for it, the fool she was, to bring the work of iniquity to nothing.

She was a fool. War just suits iniquity. But you can't live under a never-ending rumbling of thunder and savage black clouds without praying for the sky to split wide open and get it over.

Fear was in her before the bombs came. It so tightened her that when the sirens began to wail, and here it was at last, she felt relief. People everywhere had been behaving as if heated minds were epidemic. You couldn't guess what the next awful thing malignant lunacy would bring about, and each day the disease crept nearer home.

It was all over. The bad news was complete. Complete for her. The madness of men could do nothing more to her that she knew of, or cared about.

A rusty sickle was hanging by a cord from a nail over there by the window. Time's implement. A queer ornament for a bedroom. Who were the people here? Only the blue of the sky was beyond the window, under a beetling black brow of thatch. The window must frown down over a lot of empty space. A shadow darkened the window for a moment and the sparrows fled in a body. Under the window was a chest of drawers, with a cracked mirror on it tilted to reflect the ceiling, and beside the mirror was a portrait too small and faded to be a likeness of anybody.

Nothing else was there except that old almanac in front of her. It was for 1940. Yes, that year, of all the years in the past to make one positive no second experience of life is wanted! Its sheets had been turned and left at the month of May.

If there was a reminder of things gone by to make old wounds ache in the soul there before her it was, though dog-eared and fly-spotted, hanging on the wall at the foot of the bed by a nail big enough for the suspension of doom. The almanac's picture for the month, in its innocence of what it would stir up, was of London: St. Paul's from Fleet Street. A locomotive of a year out of mind was crossing the bridge above Ludgate, and the dome everybody knows was floating dramatically on a cloud of snowy steam. She saw it, one night, when London appeared to be done for, afloat on billows of raging smoke, all fiery.

May, 1940! And nobody had touched the almanac since then. Time, in this room, had stopped at the most frightful month in our history, and stood there still; the May of the tumult when France toppled over, when all Europe was down, and England tottered, while everybody waited for the last crash. Time ended then in this room, and the spiders moved in.

Yes, but did it all happen? Could it be believed? For she was cold about it now. No apprehension was left in the heart. Her head was empty. Quite empty. There was no more for her to wait for and fear. The flaming years had burned themselves out. The memory of them was gray ash. The mind can bear only so much rough use. After that, if the great globe itself should blow up, so much the better. . . .

Somebody was on their way upstairs. The slow heavy footsteps were going round a spiral ascent. She must have been far gone when she came here. She knew nothing of that stairway.

The door opened. The woman had returned, entering sideways, slowly, while delicately balancing a large cup on a small saucer.

She didn't want it, whatever it was. She couldn't look at it. She would never want to eat again. She wanted only to be left alone. That was all. Not a word from anyone. What was there to say? O God, it was true, she was alive, and she must be somewhere, with other people looking on, and they would want to help, when there was no help. The woman put the cup and saucer down by the mirror, and came and stood over her, grimly eying her, with signs of banter about her tight mouth.

"Child, if I went by your color, which you haven't got, you'd be a pretty corpse. Whoever saw eyes so bright in a body washed and laid out, as 'ee be, and I did it myself!"

She chuckled, a dry sound, and straightened the counterpane. She put the red knuckles of a gnarled fist against Lucy's cheek.

"Cool as a cabbage. I always did say city people had no blood. What be 'ee made of? Gutta-percha? Must be, after the night out you gave yourself, choosen such a cubbyhole, all draughts and rocks. Martin, he said . . ."

"Who is Martin?"

"Well, you're the one ought to know. My man of course. Martin to me and to anyone who asks."

"It was strange he should happen to pass that way."

"Nothing funny in it, so don't think it. He's drawn to it, as often as the fit takes him, when naturals go wandering. It comes of knowing the vacancy of dumb beasts. He don't have to drive un. When he shows hisself, they come. They follow on. It saves time. Here's this for you."

She went for the cup, and then sat on the edge of the bed, which sank. "You don't want it, but here I sit to see you take it. You'll have un, or we'll fall out, and my temper at home is quick and bad. It's only egg and a noggin, and you'll feel better as you lower your elbow."

"You are very good to me, but I couldn't drink it."

"Rubbish. Down with it. You've only got a maggot in your head about it. This'll shift the little devil. Go on. Shut your eyes and gulp . . . there, what did I say? That warmed 'ee, didn't un?"

Mrs. Martin, all in black, broad-based and weighty, kept her share of the bed somewhat foundered. Her eyes were narrowed in their curiosity for evidence on Lucy's face. A trifle of amused comment, light and impartial, was about her lips, and perhaps was as far as humor could ever spread on her weather-hardened features. Her eyes, and her guest noted that they were as dark and shiny as agates, and as hard, would never relent in their wariness for whatever nonsense an occasion held for her deception.

"Well, young woman, has that helped you to remember your name, which we don't know? I've a suspicion it's respectable."

Lucy smiled. "It is of no importance since my father died. He was Sir Anthony Gale."

"Was he, Miss Gale. I've never heard of him. And when did he die?"

"I don't know. What is today? . . . Friday? Then he died the day before yesterday."

"Where?"

"Budmouth."

"So that's what it comes to. Then how you managed as far as this I don't know. It beats me. I couldn't do it, except on horseback, and that would have to be Punch, our best plough horse. The others wouldn't look at me."

She laughed, shortly, like an abrupt rattle of dry sticks. "Only two days back. Young woman, you can't ever walk away from it. Only fancy, the child ignorant of what's behind us! It follows us up. It's everywhere, and it's every day for someone, of course."

Lucy mused. Ignorant of it? She did not answer.

Mrs. Martin grunted while slowly heaving herself up. She rested her fists on her hips. "Rest yourself," she said. "We'll find summat to get 'ee home, though it's awk'ard and out of place with the farm short of means."

She looked round critically. "No time to straighten up here, when Martin brought 'ee in. An' look, don't it need un! Never you mind, the bedding be as dry and sweet as herbs, anyways, and always will be, so don't worry that far, though you'd be the last to do it, from the little we've seen of 'ee."

Mrs. Martin pointed to the almanac. "There, that'll tell 'ee I'm not up here every day. No, nor in weeks. Not in use, and too many steps."

She jerked her head sideways at the insignificant portrait. "It was Bill's room, and that there sickle was his, which he kept flashy as silver and honed fine till it would flick your head off. He was that jealous of it he'd not let his father use it."

Lucy did not know what to say, but weakly ventured, "And I've been admiring the picture on that old almanac there."

"Old? Not so old. Quite new, you might say. I don't like to take un down. Let be. Only as old as Dunkirk. Don't tell me you've forgotten one day news came of Dunkirk."

"Mrs. Martin, I shall never forget it."

"That's right. I'm glad to hear someone say it. Well, that's where our Bill was last seen, and this is a quiet house."

THIRTY-FIVE

Mrs. Martin's weighty descent, while the stairs complained, diminished to silence; and Lucy, in a bottomless quiet, was left to consider further what an old almanac had to tell her. It was all she could do. There it was in front of her, the same self-existing object as before, and yet somewhat changed since a few words were addressed to it a minute ago. It had changed, as if in warning that we are never fully aware of the nature of things seen.

London's great central dome was still its spectacular reminder, counseling her that she must return to it, and at once. Yet those faded and dog-eared sheets of a time past were reproving her. She had been so possessed by her own grief, and all the while the same sorrow had been present here in this attic, part of the silence, under the dust, concealed by cobwebs. That month of May, quite out of date, had another story to tell, privately, one without any record, except fly spots. What sort of a man was Bill, who used to keep that rusty iron like silver? A tear was hesitant on Lucy's cheek, and it surprised her, and it was not for herself.

Was it possible? That the heartache she knew, the dis-

171

may at the irremediable, the yearning for what is not, is everywhere in the day's tumult, hidden, voiceless? That we only seem to be alone?

She turned her face to the window's brightness. The sparrows were back on the outside sill, shrilly confident; they had never a doubt in all they were telling each other.

She listened to them. This same light, she remembered, was in a morning room at White Stacks, and the birds were at a window then, making that same noise. Mother was with her, and had a little to say of the value of sparrows. Her attention to what was said had been dutiful.

She was told, on an authority Mother trusted, what this value was. Sparrows were quite cheap; they were two for a farthing. But they had a worth beyond, at no ruling market price, for each one had its place in the frame of existence.

Lucy recalled that her attention to those words of high authority had been listless. She was ready to run away to another matter more entertaining. The words seemed too simple to have anything in them. She told Mother so, falteringly. Mother didn't appear to expect anything different from her, but stood, still content, looking to the garden in a light as cool as truth might be, if it could be seen; and then Mother went on to say, reminiscently, as if talking to herself, that the man Shakespeare, that fellow, no less—and perhaps, she added, still smiling, I would attend to him—he, one day, had evidently been struck when reading the same words in the same book, as by a hint new and peculiar. "It is said, not a sparrow falls but it is known."

A little later that morning, when ready to depart, she picked up the portrait of Bill, to know him better. It only confused her. He wasn't exactly in it, for her. He was diminished by time's perspective far away from the use of a sickle and a rifle, as far off as a boy nursing a puppy, and the dog had moved in his arms. The portrait left no doubt that a child she had been told was Bill was nursing a dog—if it was a dog—heaven knew when. In an instant of a day without a year that dog—assuming it was one—had moved; and Bill himself, in petticoats, was a child staring at her wonderingly—his eyes were still alive—from a moment that had all but faded into oblivion.

Lucy replaced the token of a lost instant slowly and gently, as if without care the evidence would vanish utterly. It pictured Bill, no doubt, for his mother said it did, but it told her something more, and that wasn't in the picture. She saw how silly it is to try to make sense of time and what happens in it. Time is a muddle subject to accidents. That a little boy once nursed a puppy was a fact, for there the proof of it was. Yet facts, she speculated, are not the truth, after all. Lots of them may even hide the truth, unless one can see through them; and who can?

Oh dear, time doesn't seem to mean more than snapshots. It is only a succession of effort and dilemma. And cruel disappointment is added now and then for full measure, which either spurs one on, or brings one to a full stop. And like the boy in the picture, each of us suffers an hourly change; one is not quite the same creature one was yesterday. And things happen.

Never mind. Bill, who was nothing till a word conjured him up into knowledge, was Bill. Between petticoats and Dunkirk he was not to be measured by time. That wouldn't do. He was always Bill, known or unknown. Wasn't that nearer the truth than any number of snapshots? His independence of the muddle between the happy moment with his puppy, and the last sight of him in battle, was also a fact, a fact not to be recorded by any method that she knew.

Lucy was fixed, apparently lost in consideration of a remote child whose picture she had just replaced. Her hand remained on the frame of it. She was looking at it, but she did not see it. She was still by the admoniton of something above and beyond this visible limitation in which we keep busy, hardly knowing what it is we do, in a scene always changing, till we die; of a necessity unknown to us, in a timeless latitude that includes our little scope; of an unknown power infinite and pervasive, and imminent.

She recovered. She slowly turned to go. She began the descent of the crooked stairway. Her heart was lightened, if mystified. She was as certain as one can be, usually, of most happenings, that there had been a rift in the everyday scene about her. The familiar had been shaken. It did not last, yet for a moment she was aware of an unseen existence, and it was close. The usual day of effort and puzzle could be questioned. It is not all?

No, but here the familiar was again as ever. It claimed her at once. It wouldn't do to be absent-minded while exploring these twisted, narrow, darkish, unequal steps; one careful foot after another. The strange apprehension had passed. It had gone, that sense of a viewless amplitude about her; but it had left a thought to be kept. When Bill falls, is there witness? When no more than a sparrow falls, is it known? Then nothing will be overlooked. Not a thing. All is known. All is remembered. How important that must make one's own personal hour, and everything in it, even unspoken thoughts, as if judgment were present; as if eternity were now!

Old Martin greeted her in the kitchen. He put away his pipe as she appeared. "That looks better," he said. His smile would have been mocking but for his eyes.

She did not speak. She took his hand in both of hers, and they did not meet round it. He was not treelike, as she had thought, but his shoulders could be trusted to stiffen under a load. Nor was he old, though his hair was gray. Perhaps he had always been like this, a cunning, kind, and enduring man, giving the impression that Adam never died, who will put up with everything as long as is necessary.

Mrs. Martin joined them, briskly, drying her hands. "They're all fools," she exclaimed at once, "hens are, fussing up and down the run till they've found a way out of safety, but can't ever hit on it again when worry sends 'em back to join the party. Why didn't you fix that rent in the wire, Martin? I told you about it, didn't I?

175

Didn't I say it often enough? That Plymouth Rock, she's been out all night."

"She have?" said Martin. "Then say good-bye. The dun fox as big as a hound walked past the shippen this morning as if he owned us. He took no notice of me."

"Why should he?" asked his wife.

Their rallying was sharp, and Lucy knew they were acting parts, and wanted her to share the play. Sharing it was as easy as thankfulness. On the table was a bowl of water, and reflections from its trembling surface were at a jig on the wall. Sharing an intermission of comedy with these people came as easily as that dancing light. She had no reason to feel as satisfied as this, yet even the crocks on the dresser, and the brass knobs of the kitchen stove, they acted well, shining in their part of the play. There was a crisp smell of new bread. The clucking of the fowls outside was heard as a traditional undertone. She didn't know when she had last noticed the ordinary trifles of use in the home. They were good. Summer was brilliant outside, but its dazzle stopped at the porch. The kitchen was cool in transparent shadow, with residual reminders in it of earth, bread, and a sourness of fat milk.

She went out into the sun. A car for her was on its way. It had been heard, a premonition of movement in a universe that appeared to be at rest. The three waited for its approach. They were silent. There was no more to say. Before them was a rampant outpouring of light green leaves, round as coins, ardent with little flames, yellow, orange, and scarlet, and she knew again that nasturtiums are hot and smell peppery.

Over a bed of herbs, bees were darting with no time to spare, the only sign that the hour had its urgency; but beyond their small liberty with their imperative duty, down lower to where a kestrel was tremulous in suspension in vacancy, and deeper still to the expanse of the sea, and far out into the vast obscurity of summer's heat, in which a line of ships was fixed, the standing from which she viewed existence told her that time was as delusive as honey-gathering, as hope, as despair; as delusive as all except fidelity and kindness. The moment was as calm as if she had been brought to an outlook from which could be seen the splendor of an augury, serene and confiding, of a purpose inherent, but undisclosed.

THIRTY-SIX

At Bewley, it occurred to Dr. Pickles, on a tour, without haste, of the apartments of its hospital, that this was the first time in several years that he had been at liberty to do it, or had felt the desire for a solitary ramble round his charge. He took out a pocket lens to examine a plant on a window sill. How did that Alpine saxifrage get there? It was not often seen. He looked round for a nurse to tell him, but none was present.

"Have you been left to take care of yourselves?" he asked the woman in the nearest bed.

"Nurse was here only a moment ago, sir. . . . No sir, no upset this morning that I know of, or want to hear about."

The doctor went on, his mind at ease. He had the curious fancy that he was entering upon ordinary life once more, quite unexpectedly. He felt at least a lessening of the infernal tension, and that was worth having, if it was unreasonable. The aerial automata, though they continued to shock his neighborhood, were coming over in fewer numbers and at intervals more blessedly protracted. He could say that. He did not know how much longer the war would last, but he was fully satisfied that when the end came it would be in Berlin, not London; or in what was left of Berlin.

It must be in a sorry state. He was too old, or too old-fashioned, to be cheered by the certainty of retributive catastrophe. The promise of dire requital was without happiness. He had been forced too often to frowning interest over the effects on soft bodies of metal cases bursting under extravagant pressures; scrupulous care had been exacted too far in the probing of vitals mangled by intrusive objects. Retribution meant the same elsewhere. Retribution does not make amends. And here he was still at it, all the way from Gallipoli and Passchendaele to a London suburb. When an end to this snatching of life's leakage?

He paused. Ah, well. That child there. Good. She had color again though she had been drained of animation. She would play again.

"How d' do, Nancy? And how is one-eyed Teddy today? Don't cuddle him up to your mouth. He looks to me as if he ought to go to the laundry. What, you won't let him go? All right. Have it your way. He shan't go."

The spring of life must be pretty powerful in that infant. But it had been aided. He'd say for the art of healing that it was doing its best to keep up with the art of bloodshed, though he feared for the future. The handicap was impossible while destruction had first attention from authority, and more money, than the promotion of living tissue. The prevailing emphasis on the importance of each saddened him. It was his notion of sinning against the light. But there was no help for it. No help, while we are ruled by expediency. And what did that amount to? Why, just the nervous hesitancies of statesmen anxious to make a right guess at a popular cry, knowing full well the most ready instinct of the multitude is fear.

Yes, yes. Of course. Quite so. But that left out the fact that he himself said long ago, and still believed, that it would have been good for everybody if at Hitler's nativity the midwife had strangled the child. The difficulty is, the diabolic is not born with a twist of warning red cotton round a big toe. Even evil has to have its chance, nobody knows why, and never fails to use it. That meant, it was melancholy to admit, that a statesman as good as Lincoln was forced to look two ways at once while a chance like that was hanging about he never knew where.

This reflection brought him up to a shattered door, and through one of its jagged panels he looked into an empty ward. A wall within was open to the sky, the cots were occupied by rubbish, and the floor was savage with plaster and broken glass. Nothing had been done there yet. When would it be helpful again?

So welcome, victory. There was a day when one's hope of that was more forlorn than that room. Nothing was in view but ruin. When he recalled that in 1940 we were waiting for the enemy to come round the corner, the certainty this morning of his downfall at a distance was as if the utterly impossible had come about. There is a Providence which shapes our ends?

He doubted that his own faith in Providence could last three rounds with the mildest of sceptics. His guard would be weak. Yet he would rise, if groggy, at the count of nine, or what good would he be as a sawbones? To one whose anxiety had been severe, while watching, as a survivor from Ypres and the first war, a new order in Europe in the process of an ominous fermenting in Germany, it seemed fairly likely, looking back, that doom for ferocious ambition, with all its lies and treachery, so successful at first, was lurking throughout in the order of nature. Yes, there was a lot to be said for the irony of circumstance. You could easily believe that the first ugly piece of work decides concluding disaster. Full penalty was now at hand, however one looked at it.

He stopped again to examine a graph at a youth's bed,

and the boy was too awed to look up at his visitor. "That book has fixed you, Tommy. It must be good. What is it? *Monte Cristo?* Don't I wish I was in it with you?"

To his mind, it was healthful to retain a fear of Providence. It could reduce unworthy fears almost to nothing. When in doubt about your personal bias, given a questioning glance up at what you cannot see. One never knows. Who does know? Nobody knows, and that's the last word about it. It does not matter at all if dread of an overlooking from the invisible is only a survival of animism from the pagan groves, the signs of which among Christians once amused friend Nicholas. And amused him. Certainly such a fear had a line of descent. Is there anything without geniture? Suspicion that there is an eye on you, or that Providence is over all, was all to the good. It made for better manners. It seemed a pity to him that such a wholesome fear was not more widespread. How a prevalence of it would have lessened his labor in life, if also his pay!

Dr. Pickles by now was passing through a ward in which he saw Stephen and the sailor in close and alert converse. That seaman? He was leaving today, and taking with him in his interior a splinter better left where it was. It might do less harm in the long run than an uneasy conscience, so the fellow could be called sound. What were they telling each other? Young Gale had revived surprisingly. The brain and the heart had more of the toughness of aboriginal root fibers than used to be noted in the text books. Gale should do well if his wits were not knocked about abruptly too soon; he ought not

to learn what had to be known in the way a tailboard re-
leases a cartload of stones. What did that sailor know?
By the look of the man, more than he ever said, except
for its embroidery.

He eyed them. Gale had a gracious Roman sort of
head. He did not resemble his father, and if that was a
social benefit, it made him the more tender to the jolts of
fortune. Should he join in?

Better leave them alone. No meddling. The man
seemed to be interested in what the sailor was telling
him. And, however one contrives, the wind is never tem-
pered to the shorn lamb. Providence appears to be too
busy in general to attend to individual lambs. They are
left to us. He gave the pair a genial wave of his hand,
and went into his sanctum.

THIRTY-SEVEN

The Matron of the hospital, in hat and cloak, at that moment came into the corridor as if making purposefully
for Dr. Pickles' room, but changed her mind. She retired
to her own place, and was there a while before she ventured out to consult her principal.

It was inadvisable, however one was stressed, to appear informally before Dr. Pickles. His unaspiring re-

serve could not be touched to a sympathetic response. He was human, no doubt, but he never showed it unmistakedly unless absent-minded, or with children. He could be very open-hearted with a girl, if she was under the age of ten. It was unhelpful, for she suspected he understood quite well things that most men, though otherwise fully qualified, were not wisely aware made alterations in friendly and other relationships. She did not believe that in all his life he had ever let himself go. Why he chose medicine when he preferred solitude was a mystery, and perhaps a mistake.

To her surprise, Dr. Pickles, when she entered, was benign, as far as it went with him, for he gave no sign that an intrusive voice, while he was lost in consideration of whatever he had in mind, was what he never enjoyed. The day's newspapers were still in their original shape on a table. He hadn't opened them. Even the news of the day couldn't touch him. His attention had to be directed to what had happened in the world since he last fell asleep, yet the war had struck hard at his own place. You might think that all the great changes taking place everywhere were only a page or two more being added to history, which was already full, and dull, and Dr. Pickles, at this stage of it, was looking on, and wished he weren't. She supposed his apparent subnormal temperature came of a continuation of his old service in France, when she was a girl, and perhaps it was unfair to expect a man to show heartiness in the same duty so long drawn out.

She had been to Whitehall, she told him, but had

wasted her time. The woman she expected to see there was absent, they wouldn't say where. Her own sister, too. They pretended not to understand what she wanted to learn.

"What did you expect? Haven't you found out yet that the appropriate officer at Whitehall would rather admit to infamy than to knowledge, or accept responsibility for anything? Yet you've read *Little Dorrit*."

"No, I haven't. What has that to do with it?"

"You'll come to it, some day. And where do I come into it this minute?"

"I don't know whether you do. Have you seen the news today?"

"I've seen the war bulletins. That is all I know. Is there anything important beyond?"

"In a way, yes. Sir Anthony Gale is dead."

"No, I didn't know it."

"And his daughter Lucy is missing."

Dr. Pickles looked up sharply. "Eh? What's that? What has happened?"

"I wish I knew. There were a few lines in one paper about it, that's all."

The doctor took up a magnifying glass from his table, and turned it about, as though for its possible application to the indistinction of this further item of news in time of war. He put it down.

"Missing? What does it mean? Both together in an accident?"

"I've told you all I know, and I don't know what it means."

They were silent for a space, looking elsewhere than at each other for a clue to the unexplained.

"What is there we can do?" asked the Matron. "I don't know to whom to send, nor where to send, and I must do something. The family has disappeared, except the patient here. It is terrible. Lucy was the daughter of one of my dearest friends. She was often here, with her mother. They were very helpful to me."

"She was a very bright little woman. I've seen her about, when I was with Nicholas—you know, Dr. Tregarthen—up at the house."

"Her mother had the last word for me, when I felt somebody had to be consulted."

"I understand," said the doctor. "I've heard that Sir Anthony's wife was a kind and sagacious lady."

"Yes, she was. She was more than that. And now this. I have seen her concern for her daughter. Lucy had odd impulses, one didn't know why, and she must have given her mother some fretting. I was fond of that girl. She was so likable, yet one was kept from approaching her."

"I noticed she had a lively and candid wit. I should have called her self-sufficient. She could hold her own with her uncle, and not many could do that. But I seldom saw her. Nor her mother. When I was at White Stacks it was Nicholas. You know the man I mean."

"I've heard about him."

"Many had heard about him, but not many knew him. The others up there I didn't know as well as I should. I cannot recall young Gale about the house, though I must have seen him, must have seen him. It's him I'm thinking of now."

"It's a dreadful complication. I don't believe he knows what happened. He hasn't asked a question. It's so queer. How can he be told this? He gives me the impression that he supposes he is the family victim, and is waiting for his people to come in any minute. Past time to him is perhaps what it was to Rip Van Winkle. I've warned that fellow in the next bed about it. What are we to do? A word at the wrong moment may wipe out the Gales."

"It may. And we might as well try to hold up a phase of the moon."

"I owe so much to Lady Gale . . ."

"There is nothing we can do, that I can see, except leave it to another twist of chance, and see what happens. If nobody visits him, a question may grow in him. Curiosity will overcome his present languor. There we must leave it. And a missing person is found, sometimes."

"Leave it? How can we leave it? Leave the man to chance?"

"Whatever we do at the moment may be wrong."

The Matron turned hesitatingly, about to go, but was restrained by a further doubt. She fidgeted with her reticule. There was no more to be said, and nothing to be done, except wait for the next turn of fate. To wait . . . !

Dr. Pickles pushed back his chair, went to the window, saw nothing outside to keep him, so stood at the fireplace, his back to his suppliant. He appeared to be studying a pleasant old engraving on the wall. It was of

Bewley's medieval church, in which the Gales were commemorated. Above the church on the hillside, the picture just showed White Stacks distant within a dark cloud of trees.

"It isn't there," Dr. Pickles told himself, and loudly. "We have seen the last of that house."

He turned to the lady in his room, though he did not look at her, but at whatever was beyond where she stood. "We may save our young patient," he said, "but what the Gales meant, what that household was in English life, that has gone. We must say so. It is lost."

He was restless, and wandered about. "There was friend Nicholas, erudite for the fun of it, individual in eccentric devilment—you don't know, do you, that he added a little of his own to surgical knowledge, as well as to scandal?—no more of his sort. There's no place for it. There's no use for the likes of him. We distrust people unlike ourselves. All to be of one mind feels safer than freedom. This is the day of everybody, one sort of life, and the Gales and Nicholas are done."

The Matron opened her eyes, and for a moment lost the sense of immediate tragedy. She had never before known Dr. Pickles to lose himself like this. "I'm so sorry," she faltered. "I never knew your friend. I don't think he ever spoke to me."

"What? It isn't that. One's friends go. That is a penalty for getting on in years. It isn't that. There is nothing new in the loss of an old friend. What is new is the extinction of a quality in the body of English life. That's the trouble. I don't know how to put it."

He dropped his glass, and then held it up to the light, as if this lack of perspicacity were in it. "Those people who used to be at the house on the hill. You knew their place. You've been there. I mean homes of the Gales' sort, dotted about this Island in all its shires, with elements almost as old as the underground rocks. Such a house as theirs, with its own spirit, its own promptings. You see what is happening, don't you? It is clear enough, if you look back, if you look round."

He stopped and contemplated the old engraving. "It was those characters who brought about the common temper which gave this country a name with power. I don't mean guns. No. Ideas. The ruins where White Stacks used to be—have you been up there lately?—weeds have begun to cover it up—that wreckage is only a sign of a general going off. Yet they were the sort of people who hammered out notions of government for everybody, and the sparks flew about. Took hold, too. Don't you know, they caught light to the various great revolutions elsewhere. France and America. This land was the anvil. The law is what they made it. They wrote the best we have on our bookshelves. They turned the Scriptures into pages that could be read in cottages, and gave us a way of speech. They began the State, and shaped it. They ran it. Got rid of kings who would not fit in. The pith and marrow of those families is our tradition. They led in war, and this war ends them. Their day is over."

The Matron, in quietude, appeared not to heed him, except politely, and the doctor said no more. He could have been regretting already that he had been talking when words were of no avail, except to reveal that he was just as liable as the weak-headed to betray in wayward speech the secrets of the heart.

He went to the window again and looked out, as to the light of a new era, for what signs showed in it, so far, of new shapes to take the place of old good things that were gone beyond recall. Then he heard behind him a sound, though it was but faint, a little noise which always perplexed him, and chilled his spirit. The Matron was deeply grieving. He had upset her.

He nervously adjusted his glasses. "I'm afraid I've not been speaking by the book," he assured her. "Events have stressed us, and then words break out with no compunction."

She sank into his chair, no longer able to suffer eloquence while standing, and she did not care whose chair she took. Her hands covered her eyes. She spoke with a little difficulty. "It—it isn't that—not what you said." She began to laugh, still covering her eyes, her head thrown back. Untimely merriment was beginning to possess and shake her.

The doctor hurried to a cupboard, but the mere clinking of the vials restored his visitor.

"I don't want that," she called out. "I'm quite all right. It was nothing. I've been too busy in a hurry, that is all, and nothing done."

She sat upright stiffly, and waved away the glass he offered. She smiled. "That won't cure all that you've been telling me."

Dr. Pickles brightened. "No, there's no cordial for it. We cannot give it help. It is dismissed. We will attend to what can prosper."

The Matron rose. She was composed, and was still smiling, if wanly. "It wasn't what you said. I suppose you are right. We have lost all that. But it gave the last touch, and my balance went. I'd been thinking this morning that the world has turned upside down, and my eyes aren't used to it."

"So it has, but we'll get used to it."

"No. I mean it. I saw it go high in the air and turn over."

Dr. Pickles' bushy eyebrows went up, dubiously.

"The nonsense at Whitehall," she explained. "That began it. I came away furious with myself for having tried to reason with Bedlam. In the car, on the way here, scanning a newspaper, I saw that paragraph—Sir Anthony and Lucy. Then I began to turn the paper over and over in a hurry for what it wouldn't tell me. While I was doing that it happened. Somewhere near the Elephant and Castle. The car jumped and stopped. I thought we had run into a wall which wasn't there. A policeman was all I saw, holding out his arm. The air was shaking like a jelly, and so was I. Ahead of us a car ran out of a garage. It rose into the air above the tram lines, a bird of a car in a dream. It went up and up to turn a slow somersault in reverse, quite gay, as high as the houses, and came down neatly on all fours on a roof, and disappeared. Into a bedroom, I suppose. The roof erupted like a volcano, but I must have been deaf, or fast asleep. Nothing moved but the car, and then the roof. I heard the tiles when they crashed on the pavement, and that woke me. The policeman's arm fell at the same moment, like the signal for us to get going, and we did. Everybody. Everywhere. Stampeded."

"Yes?" asked the doctor.

"Oh, one of the rockets. We heard about it afterwards while finding a way round what it had done. They're awful, those new horrors, but they have one good point. Nobody hears them coming. One of them arrives while the policeman's arm is up, and if you feel the air shuddering, you've come through. . . . Our dear Cockney chauffeur will have a nice tale to tell of me. It will just suit his style. For the first time since it all began I cursed the Germans. Better than I thought I could. I let myself go."

"That was the only thing to do. You'll be the better for it. It had to come. You've been wanting to do it for years . . . To curse them. To curse them."

The Matron made to depart, and the doctor accompanied her. "But this has struck me," he said, as he opened the door for her. "This very hour in a shelter under the ruins of Berlin is the famous man who said proudly, not long ago, that he would give Europe a shape that would last a thousand years. As he listens for further news of his luck, he hears of collapse at Stalingrad. The bell tolls for Germany. He hears it, and presently he will hear the Russian guns. No cursing will make that fellow feel worse than he does."

They stood in the corridor, and Dr. Pickles was turning to re-enter his room, but was stayed by the sight of another visitor, at the end of the passage, approaching them. The Matron exclaimed. Lucy Gale was in Bewley.

THIRTY-EIGHT

The sailor was sitting beside Stephen's bed, fiddling with his cap, when Dr. Pickles was passing, and had paused to question his patient's ability to listen without harm.

The sailor was saying to Stephen, "You had such a pinched nose. Like putty. I thought you were giving us the slip. Now you look nearly in shape for the muster."

"I'm fine," said Stephen, sitting up readily. "Nothing amiss here."

"You wait for orders. Only duffers rouse before they hear the shout."

"But you're nursing your cap. Why?"

"I'm pushing off."

"Leaving us?"

"Today."

"Then how shall I find you? I shall want to. Where are you pushing off to?"

"How should I know? I never know till I'm there. And where is it?"

"I say, surely the place matters? You want to know where you are going, don't you?"

"Not me. Not now. If I bar anything it's winter, Western Ocean. I've had all I want of that, on a low freeboard. You know what I mean. The wind like perishing death, and water as big as the end of everything falling inboard and no time to move. I don't fancy it."

"Why not choose a high freeboard?"

"Listen to him. Choose, says he. High, or a foot above the fathoms, you take what's there. What's more, make the best choice you know, and come full tally it turns out to be as good as a hole in an empty mess kit. Then where are you? So always leave it alone. Take what comes, and it'll come soon enough, dammit."

"You don't want a shore job?"

"I don't? Do I not! That's all. Only that. It's a sailor's dream in the middle watch. But would I keep it? That's the question. My eyes wouldn't take to it. I should muck what I was doing while looking to the offing, which would be only a factory wall always for keeps. At the end of the watch, no break of day. I don't want to get short-sighted . . . You can laugh. It's nothing to laugh at." The sailor spun up his cap, and caught it.

"I believe I know what you mean," said Stephen.

"That's the way you'd see it. Some chaps do, but mostly they don't. Women never see it."

Stephen gave the sailor a sly glance. "Your wife doesn't like it?"

"Like it or lump it, she isn't there. Not yet. Though I've been as near to it as a cold sweat. I will be again, if I know myself, and perhaps I do."

This little digression left them in vacancy, till the sailor looked about him, and rallied. "You know, I don't blame the women. The sea isn't common sense. And between ourselves, a woman always wants you to be in the place where you were last. That's another thing. That's where a man belongs, where he's been put. The girls don't understand what they can't turn the key on, and keep till wanted. But there's no lock for the way the wind blows. One day a tide rises above the kitchen, and off you float. . . . You're laughing easy today. What's funny in that?"

"Nothing. Did I laugh? It was what you said. I saw something far away, as you spoke. It came as you spoke. Where's the Dodman? You said float off, and I did. I was off there one night, clear dark, no wind, and a great swell running inshore; and I was alone. I was next to the water. It was up to the cockpit coaming."

"Here. You? Single-handed in a little thing?"

"I suppose so. No. Someone was with me, but I can't see them now. Who was it? The sky was full of stars, and the shore lights told me to keep off when I didn't know if I could. It was my show. I had to do it. I had never seen anything so grand in my life. I felt as good as two men."

"Then you're fine. That's the way to talk. No wind, and a westerly swell meant something was going to blow up soon. But you made it. Must have made it, for here you are."

"Yes, but what do I know?"

"What I said, and it's a fact. You know what most of 'em never will, not in old age. Those chaps can't learn. They're closed in. They're the fellers who say we're off the rails if we don't keep to the same old macadam, the one they walk. It's all they know. We're the queer boys, to push off, like you did. Why, I've sighted Dodman Point, bound out, and the farther off the better. It's a lee for the finish, in the weather you had. There's a search alongshore next day. Sailor unknown. And that reminds me. Those fellows say the sea is a horrible place, and so it is. Off and on it's all that, especially on nights when you can hear more than you can see. I've said so. I've said it every time I've been back in a chair with only a half-crown clock on the mantelpiece among the photographs and china dogs. The trouble for me is, the street has no ship's bell. There's no call from the lookout. In an early light, you can't see a new landfall when the heave of the waters lifts you up."

"You cannot," said Stephen.

"No. So we're getting there, it's in sight. We've both seen it to prove we're coming along. The sea, that old gamble, that isn't all the story, but there it always is, open wide for everybody, and you keep topside out there if you know how, as well as being lucky. There's no common sense in it. The sea's not good, and it's not a wicked old devil's own like a few people I've met. It's only the sea. Sometimes you have to make a quick move

195

on it, and only the sky knows if you brought it off; or if you didn't. You jump the right way when there's no time for it, or there's more room on the mess bench. It's the sea. You keep on facing what's there when you're as lonely as the last bird on a mudflat at low water, and the sun nearly gone. That's how it is. But you know who you are. You know that. And you get more light out there at sunup, more miles to look round on, and the tune you whistle as you pass the galley . . . Look here Mr. Gale, if I were you I'd straighten out. You better lie down. Don't sit up and look at me that way. I ain't done nothing. You lie down. You haven't got to turn out yet."

Stephen obeyed. He was smiling. "I know. I can see who was down below that night. It was Lucy. Of course it was. She used to think we were done for when we weren't, yet she would come. To take care of me, I suppose. I say, don't you know, we may see my sister today? You haven't met her, but you'll see her soon."

The sailor let fall his cap. He was more than leisurely when recovering it. This needed time. Would they see her soon? Who knew what to expect, these days? It was more than a week since she had been there, as well as he remembered. He hadn't seen the old man, either.

"Is her name Lucy?" the sailor asked, looking up. "Why, I knew a Lucy once. That was before I had much sense. Perhaps I hadn't any then. It doesn't look like it. Her father kept the Spotted Dog just outside Gravesend. I took a shore job because of that girl, just to be able to drop in and watch her at the beerpulls. They were ebony with silver bands. They had a way of bowing into the soft bulge of her buttons, and it made me envious. She wasn't like the others, so I thought. That was the girl got me to sign on for a voyage and a half. Didn't I ever tell you?"

"No," said Stephen.

"Then here goes."

THIRTY-NINE

Do you know Gravesend? You do and all. Everybody knows it that ever heard the call of a ship, and answered it, once too often. The Spotted Dog was a ready-for-you local, except when there were too many toughs about just paid off. Then Lucy was busy. But, from a bench outside, at the turn of the tide, you could see all the bunting of the world go by in the wind, so the girl at the beerpulls inside didn't matter all that much. Come to think of it, it puzzles me how I kept to the shore so long, mixing cement, that lively mud, when the masts and funnels were on the move down there cutting across the open end of the street. Though you didn't know my Lucy, and never will, and that's your luck.

Her father, old Trinder, he'd done well as a ship's master. He did well after he had picked up a deep freighter that had dropped her propeller, and towed her into port.

That was salvage. It's the only way left to make money at sea, so I'm done. I shall never see any. But Trinder was a man a foot or more taller than his money. He left the work to Lucy and her maid and the potman; and it's my idea that Lucy knew the liquor and the measures in a way an exciseman ought not to. Her father put in most of his day by the water front, with the Trinity House men, just like you would. Like I would have done, with more sense.

The old man had a way with him, and I kept clear of it as well as I could. I was shy, those days, and he had a big manner and a strong voice that had grown powerful on him at the poop rail when he had command, so he couldn't help it. Then one day he found me out. I let drop I knew a bit. It surprised him that I knew what outboard channels were—you don't know what they were so don't say you do, and they don't matter, anyway—and that brought me next to him.

"How do you know that?" he said, as stern as if I had annoyed him. Then he took my arm. He hauled me into his parlor, and filled my can. He didn't go to the Pilot Station that day. I was good enough for him, and promoted. He talked of the good old days, the way old men do, and it's no good blaming them, as if the sun had gone dim over the likes of us since better men used to eat cracker hash because that was all the grub they could get. You'd have thought that once he'd sighted heaven's gates, there they were, and he knew it, but he couldn't land because of the surf. Those were the days.

He knew ships, anyway, in a style owners never do.

He learned the ropes on the *Sir Lancelot*. She was one of the fliers home from China, according to him, and beat the fleet. If your nerves weren't up to it, then keep away from her when she was doing her best, so he said. Old Trinder went on like that, but at last shook his head, and sighed, and he grew sorrowful enough for the tears to drop into his beard.

He admitted that in those days, when he was better off than he knew, he was a fool. He used to think, on nights that had broken loose in the dark, and were pouring off the earth in a flood, hove-to in an uproar he couldn't see, that the sensible thing was to run a pub, quiet and warm, like this one, and do that for the rest of his days. Live in a hulk that kept still at an anchorage, with a bed to sleep in that wasn't the wash slopping over your face. It's natural to think you'd be better off doing what you ain't. Old Trinder said he had the fancy, in his time at sea, that beer engines in a Thames-side local would be a simple rig, and you couldn't make a wrong turn with it, nothing to dismast you.

Now he knew he was right. He had it, and it was too simple. That was what made him sad. The worry of not knowing what was going to happen next had gone out of his day, and soon he'd be too old to care. That's how it was. Yet he did make a wrong turn, all widdershins, just the same, before it was too late to do it. So did I. One day, Lucy was confidential with me, and it made me feel better than I am. We were alone, and she leaned on the bar across to me, to speak low, so that I couldn't help noticing the moulding of her throat, which was the whitest

I'd seen till then, and more than her throat. Her forget-me-not eyes kept on mine, as if there was a secret between us, and we knew each other, and there was no need to mention it.

She told me how worried she was. It was about her father. Had I noticed, she asked, one of the Tames penny paddle steamers at the buoys?

Well, I had, the day before, just as you'd notice anything out of the ordinary, where ships are. I had seen the rusty curiosity, because it was there. What of it?

"Father's going to own it," she said. She took her eyes off me, which made me look at hers more concerned.

"What for?" I said. "What's the good of it? There's nothing for it to do, and nowhere for it to go."

"There is," she said. "He must be mad, unless he brings it off."

"Brings off what?"

"I'll tell you presently," she said, as a customer came in. I thought he was only a customer, but she took him round, and not a word said, to the back of the house, and left me; and I didn't like the man, who was got up in a way that would have made me feel I had gone too far in collars, though it suited him. But I am only a sailor, and he wasn't, though I think I know a shark when I see one.

So I strolled down to the pier, and wasn't sure I'd ever go back to the Spotted Dog, unless I wanted to. I was still wondering who that fellow was, and why he was, just as you've wasted a nice day, now and then, because you wanted to know what you will never know, and would feel no better if you did. Then a loud voice brought back the river right before me, all alive.

"What are you doing here, mister?" It was old Trinder.

Feeling as I did, I told him I was doing nothing that I wanted to do, and was thinking about a ship again.

He put on a quarter-deck air, screwed his eyes and fingered his beard, and he looked me over. "What about your discharge?"

"Mine? Why, I could show mine to the P and O Shore Superintendent across at Tilbury, and be damned to him, and the admiral at the Nore."

"Then come with me and have a look," he said. "We're just going."

So I went, though I didn't know where we were going. That came later. Much later. The wherry brought up by a sponson of the penny steamer, and on it we clambered, with a few other fellers who were nothing to me. I didn't count them.

She was bigger than she had looked, and better done. It was only her paint that was bad. Her engines had been cared for. They looked as if they ought to go when started. I'll say that for engineers. They take more care of boilers and bearings than they do of their own insides. I noticed how she was, not much interested, while wondering why I was there. Old Trinder had a lot to say to the others, but nothing to me; not till we were ashore again, and by ourselves.

"Well, she's mine. What about her? What do you want to say?" he said.

"She ought to hold together," says I, "from here to Greenwich, and back again. Bring it off next day, too, I shouldn't wonder."

"No more? There's a surveyor tells me she's good for a run to Rio d'Oro."

"All that? Is she though? But where's this Rio place? I don't know it."

"West Africa. I must get the charts. I haven't fixed it yet."

"Africa? You'll want more than charts, won't you, for that? I'd want that surveyor to ship with me. His view of it might help to float her across the Bay."

"That's work for a seaman," Trinder mumbled. "It's not what I'm paying him for."

The old man looked down his nose, though, as if he'd just seen a fly on it. "If I could tie her up at that place," he said, "and nothing started in her, there'd be a lot in it. Besides, it's something to do. That's what I'm thinking of, and there's my money on it, to keep me at it."

I never know what to say when a superior officer makes a mixed noise like that, so I told him there ought to be money in it. If he brought it off, it was more than anybody else in Gravesend could do.

The old man straightened himself. "I've done as much before. Look here, mister. I've an idea. You've got the right cut for this outfit. I want you. You better see this surveyor. He'll tell you how things are. He ought to be at the Spotted Dog now."

I didn't tell Trinder I knew the fellow was there, but said I'd think about it, and be along soon. Then I went for a walk, and made it a long one. I wasn't going to be talked into folly at sea by anyone who wore such a colored waistcoat. Somebody had money in the game already, very likely, or was getting some out of it; and I'd been in ships long enough to know that a sailor is the man to put his foot in a land trap that a parson would step over without noticing it. Poor Captain Trinder. Though after all, what's the good of being a sailorman if your ship doesn't come before all the life you've got? I couldn't help liking the old boy for that. He could still back his judgment, while he conned his job, against any weather he met.

That made it easy for Lucy, when I saw her afterwards. I was the same as her old father. I was only another blessed sailor. Any time she met my eyes, I thought I'd surprised her as the boy she'd always been looking for, and never expected to find. She said she wouldn't ever have agreed to the gamble if she couldn't have had my promise to stand by Dad. I was the only one in the bunch she could trust to hold on. And did I know the ship had been renamed? Yes, it had been. It was *Lucy*, after her.

Now what could I do, after that? I did what you or any other fool would have done. I went.

I don't know where our craft's load line was, because we stowed coal wherever it wouldn't upset her lopsidedness. We were not regular seamen. We were only boat-runners, the sort of chaps who'll engage to tow a sawmill to any port on earth where it's wanted, when there's nothing else to do, and serve the fools right if they drown for the money in it. The *Lucy's* runners must have signed on as Billy Bloodybones his mark, and you'd have said so, but you were safe with them. They only laughed. And one fine Sunday evening Ushant light was abeam, and the *Lucy's* paddles kept flogging her along into the Bay as easy as if we were heading for Cherry Garden Pier. She was built on the Clyde. You could say that for her, and she knew it herself.

We had no complaints, except that a beam swell would sink our paddle box, and put the other free in the air, and then you'd fancy she would flog herself apart; but she held her course. I was thinking that *Lucy* was a good girl, and the sea naturally was kind to a child. We were doing fine. We were in luck. As for Trinder, if he wasn't as good a man out of a home port as ever took a ship south along the Portuguese coast looking for trouble, or making it, then I've wasted my time afloat. We kept close in, in case, but even when somewhere west of St. Vincent, and she was under a black sky that nearly scraped her upperworks, and was flung about like a barrel in a cataract, when her engines sounded to me like ironmongery on the spree, her master only squeezed the water out of his hairy face so he could see better in the dark. Besides, her engineer was a Londonderry man, Pete Curran, so he knew a riot full and loud and no police usually means no more than a sober next day feeling a little sore.

We kept well away from Africa. Often its landmarks are only lies in a fog just when you think you've fixed the right one, and the great rollers sweeping towards what isn't there would make you think the sea floor itself was a carpet with a gale blowing under it. A mistake on that coast, and you're soon forgotten. But Trinder made his landfall to the minute, though I saw nothing for a long time after the *Lucy* turned east, except the skyline was growing short hairs, which were palms.

We entered the Rio d'Oro that evening, and anchored. What would come next in that place, by the best we could see of it, wasn't worth a guess. It was too hot and steamy to think, anyway; and to grouse because you're in such a hole in a bad light only makes more sweat. Anyway, it's always sense to leave tomorrow alone. That'll come whether you're there or not. The only fact, and it didn't help much, was a sudden outburst of noise from the forest everywhere as we got in, and the sun went. The branches nearly met over the *Lucy*. She was in a tunnel, and an orchestra struck up there. It was our welcome, and it was close. I didn't know the instruments. They were new to me. I thought the nightmares of that place were prancing out of their stables under the roots of the trees, when they saw us, and got going on steam whistles, knife grinders, and anything else so sharp that you knew you were deep in the foreign, and had all to learn. But it switched off while we wondered what the devil it was. There we were, and in a minute the silence was midnight and no bottom to it.

Next morning the voyage really began towards that wharf where we would tie up our *Lucy*, and see our money. We began to wind about deeper and deeper into the forest. Soon we found out that Africa only stands over you day after day, not caring what you say or what you want, because it goes on for ever and ever, and you can't. Each sunset came none of us knew where, and left us in the dark. The sun always went down exploding through the total wreck of the sky, and our deck had the reflections of the last day to show up our faces and small size, and we knew all we had done in working time had got us nowhere.

Trinder told us, for the men began to speak up strong enough to hear fore and aft, that the end of our voyage was some way up river yet. We had to put up with a few more of this sort of thing. Patience, boys, patience, and soon we'll meet the agent, fix a return home, and all's well; but our destination wasn't on the map, he said, and never had been.

You could see it wasn't. He had to look for it. We were right off the map. We should know where we were when we arrived. Of a morning, as we got under way again, our cable made the first noise ever heard there in daylight. The slow black water was still there, the forest walls close and high to port and starboard, and ours the only movement since trees were made. Nobody else was in that place, or we hoped not, and the stink stirred up by the paddles from what was rotting under us stuck in the throat; and monkeys were aloft, and the nobs that were the eyes and snouts of crocodiles were afloat like corks, and there the sun was again over the roof of the forest to bow us down. But we held on. Pete Curran said, "You should know what heat is like by the boilers, but the devil has nothing on me, for when the coal's gone there's more wood about than they've got in hell—Glory be to God!"

What a wharf would be doing on that river, I gave up asking myself. I couldn't ask Trinder. He had enough on hand easing us over stretches where the mud and our draught just about met. It seemed to me he was overdoing it. He was looking grayer than his age. But there was no letup for him, as he was the pilot where soundings had to be made for the first time; he must do it himself, or be lost, and he had nobody to ask, except when he saw himself in the mess room mirror, which was cracked. He had let a fancy work on him, while peaceful at home, and this was what it came to, so far, and he had brought us with him.

Early one morning, just as the shape of things began to come through, I was on deck, getting a mouthful of what cool air was left before the sun was up. I was peering at what was hard to make out alongside, shapes I wasn't sure were real, and a tangle of ropes hanging down before me from the trees to give fits to a ship's rigger, and not a whisper anywhere. We were right back into old once-upon-a-time, and I was wondering how I was to get out of it. We had some sick. The rot and the heat were working on us. Something moved down there, by the edge of the water, and with a stare I made it out. A leopard was poking his big round head through the raffle of leaves, drinking. He stared up at me, when he had had enough, as if I was a cockroach, and dissolved.

There was a chuckle beside me. Pete Curran was up, and sharing it. "Did ye see that now?" he said. "That was the face of it. Now we've seen the eyes it has. I didn't know this place had a face, and its eyes put you into loneliness. Come away down, and I'll find a bottle."

Said he to me, when he found two tin mugs, "Another day of this, and I'll be firing her with wood. Now you know more than the Old Man, for he's that weak it would be dangerous to warn him in a sudden minute. He'd think it was too much to ask of a home-loving ship heading for the middle of Africa, and in his soul he'd suppose he'd been the death of her, instead of a good husband. He's more than her owner. She's his last command. It's his pride. But she'll run. She'll do it. Here's to that wharf we're after, and may we see it tomorrow! We need it, for I've the beginning of a fear myself . . .

"Eh? The engines, you say? They were not built for what they've done, but I know the shop that turned them out, and they're faithful. It's not that. It's this endless land, and the power of it, and the smell of it. My father never told me, and he was up the Niger when young, so I didn't know till I woke up here what sun and rain have it in them to do. Only the two of them, and nothing but common dirt to work on. Fermenting dirt, and ye've seen the expansion they give it, with its smell of eternal guano for perpetual motion.

"Then will you tell me this. Is this same power lying in wait, think you, under our streets at home, and the railways and factories, and the local lodges of the sons of freedom? Now, could it ever rot and cover up all we've been busy on, think you, and away with fools in their pride and folly? I'm fearing the conjecture. I'm remembering on this river, when off watch, that good man Father McCotter. He's gone now, he's sunk in the years. But when I was young and boastful, and feared nothing, I'd be telling him of the power of a new great job we were at on the shipyard benches. That was Belfast. It was the *Titanic*. I've been thinking of what that parish priest, and he was gray and gentle, said of the high pressure and speed we were after. 'You and your marvelous horsepower,' he said. 'It is your engineer's ignorance, prideful of your presumptuous formulas,' said he, 'but there's more power beyond, and in wait, and no formula for it in your books, and never will be and you'll be the clever boy, striking matches against the eclipse.'

"So I don't know as much as I did, being older. I have suspicion of my ignorance, when fiddling with what isn't there but will be. Here we go, digging away so gay into facts for our fine job, but there's no slide rule for where it will land us. If by chance we overdo it? If we cut out life line? Why, then, it may be that those who were high and mighty, and those like us in this cabin this day, won't be known to the worms. . . . Will you have another? No? Well, 'tis early yet. I'll to the gauges. She shall run."

Next afternoon it was and we were rounding a bend, tearing down leaves and wasps' nests over us. We were scraping the land so close it would make a ship give up, and back out; all the same as the other bends, no change

209

in the river, and somebody shouted. We crowded the rails.

We were there. This was it. Our port had met us. It had a name board, in case we missed a deep hole in the tangle. Our whistle blew, to wake 'em up ashore.

The whistle shook some vultures out of a skeleton tree. When the echoes of the whistle faded out, I tell you I'd never heard a silence drop plumb as heavy as that before, that's right, nor seen nothing so far off as that place. The Rio d'Oro Mining Company. We tied up. We didn't say much to each other. We kept our eyes on a shed ashore, to see somebody come out of it. Nobody came.

Only the bareboned tree and a shed were in the clearing. I went ashore, with two of the hands. There was a smell in the shed, and a packing case. At the far end of the shed was a black hiding place, but I couldn't find anything in it, and didn't want to. An empty bottle stood on the packing case. It had been used before, I don't know when, and left very likely because somebody might come along, and he'd want to have a light in Africa. Not me. I made for the ship. It was too quiet, and the forest too close. And Trinder, he'd be waiting for news.

He was pretty limp that day. He couldn't go himself, so he sent me. He said he could only trust me and Pete Curran for facts. I took them to him, and it was a light freight and a rotten job. When I went into his cabin he was flat out, and his eyes closed. His face told me the Spotted Dog was too far off to reach. I didn't know whether I'd see it again myself, but I didn't think much about it, anyway. The Old Man opened his eyes, and lifted on one elbow as I came in and shut the door. "Well?" he said.

So I told him. It didn't take a minute. He fell flat again, and I thought I'd done enough to kill him.

I didn't like to leave him. There was nothing more to talk about, either, not with a quiet man who was only waiting for what was to come with his eyes wide open on the ceiling. I did do a bit of thinking. This was the end of the charter, but I couldn't tell the Skipper I felt blue, and I couldn't break away. Time weighed a ton on me, but there was nowhere to put it. Then the Old Man spoke.

"You still here? Very well. That will do," he said.

I was glad to be off, and was opening the door when he spoke again. "Wait," he said, so I did.

"I know what you are thinking," he said, still looking at the ceiling. "Confound these flies," he said, "they're too soon," and he brushed them off his face. "You're thinking this is a total, the ship ashore. She isn't. She's sound. Pete and you will get her free. There's a Portuguese settlement north of this river's mouth, and her price will get you home. Go ten miles southwest from the river to clear before you steer north. You know the chart. I can do no more. That's all."

It wasn't all. Presently his whiskers began to move as he muttered to himself. I went nearer. Somebody might want to know what he said.

"They'll talk," he was saying. "I can hear them.

They'll talk. They said I'd never do it. Warned me off. I'd like to see them again . . . No more. Arrivals and departures off the pier, the ships will come and go, but no signal from me. I'd never do it, so they said. But I did it. She's here. That condemned penny steamer, no insurance, Thames to West Africa, she's here. I brought her out, and she's here, and not a bolt started in her. Why not? I knew I could. They'll never know, though. . . . Why are you standing there, you? What are you waiting for?"

"I'll tell them," I said.

"You? Who are you? It wouldn't help. There's nothing to show. It doesn't matter. I tell you it doesn't matter. Let them have the tale they like. I know what I know, and it's enough. It's enough, at the end."

The sailor examined his cap, as if his interest flagged. He meditated for so long that Stephen sat up, expectant.

"But afterwards?" asked Stephen. "You went to Gravesend afterwards? You told Lucy?"

"Told her? No, I haven't seen her since. I'm telling you. New people at the pub. She'd gone."

FORTY

The sailor stretched his arms, and yawned. His eyes went to the clouds beyond the window. His lazy movement, in safe repose, prompted Stephen back into the inexorable present. It was the end of a passage. There was no more to say.

The white wall of the hospital ward was suddenly there, with its familiar picture opposite Stephen's cot, that odd pattern of flagrant colors without a meaning, as well as he knew. He eyed it, but his compassionate thought for tragic failure long ago was still with him. Poor Trinder! The unlucky man! Lost, far from the Argive land! Success came to him, and defeat with it. What did that mean?

He looked round the ward to be sure of himself. He couldn't help a lurking doubt over which was the dream, and which the business in hand, for the things of the insistent present made that ship's master, remote and forsaken, the more appealing.

The Matron stood at the distant door, Nurse Bridget beside her, both seriously watching him and his companion. Why? He forgot them. A patient began to cough. The chap across the way was reading a book.

These little things, and the clock telling the time of day, deepened in his mind the distance of what was, all the sad past with its lost endeavor, and what is, the unwitting now.

"How awful," he exclaimed.

"What's awful?" asked the sailor.

"To end like that. Out there, in that place, his effort broken."

"What, my Old Man? Well, it's to come, isn't it? Some time, some place or other, some way. You can't pick the bearings for it."

"No. But abandoned in that country, his good work unremembered."

"What's the odds? The sea floor is littered with us. Where's the mark for that?"

"No mark. Nor in the desert places."

The sailor made a wry face. "Every hole and corner of the earth, so let's wash it out. There was Trinder. He liked company. Every Sunday morning at eight bells he'd have the crowd in his cabin for drinks and a gossip, to keep things sweet. You could call out a rough joke to him then, unless you were afraid of him. He had an eye for duffers. Now look at it. Who goes now? Nobody ever will. Perhaps of an evening a party of chimps stops by, making funny faces at the cross we put up, if it's still there."

"I don't like it," said Stephen.

"Who does? It won't add up, and never would, so don't let's try. It's no worse, is it, than what's going on now, every minute of the week, outside? What about that?"

"It isn't."

"That's right, and we're topside. We're here."

"We're here. All the same, your captain's story sticks in me. He let all go, and went away to do what he thought ought to be done, and what happened? It came to nothing. You told me his own daughter doesn't know."

The sailor chuckled. "He got no promise about a lovely tombstone with some nice words on it. Didn't occur to him, I suppose. But I think of him, off and on. He's a safe mark to go by. I'll bet Pete Curran don't forget, either, if he's still about, and now you know. The Old Man set out on a job he couldn't do, nor nobody else, and did it. He brought it off, and he paid for it. What came after couldn't be helped. It's enough. He was right, and that settles it. It doesn't matter where his bones are, if any."

Stephen closed his eyes on this, to consider it, and appeared to be content. He was at rest. Then a man, as he saw it, unsure of his place and part, could do no more than offer himself in the sanctuary of his choice, freely, without reserve, expecting no reward, asking no favor, trusting that good would be served. Now if he went a mile down to dig a few tons of coal, or could rise to one good poem, wouldn't that do? That was all. This sailor here knew a lot more than he did, and thought nothing of it.

The sailor shuffled to his feet. Going, was he? Stephen

did not want him to go, not yet, and stretched out a hand, absently, to stay him.

"Visitors," warned the sailor. "Here's your Lucy coming."

He remained on his feet, as if, politely, he would now retire; but what really held him was that, in a moment of strict attention, the woman he saw swiftly approaching them gave that severe apartment an air of strange excellence, and he hadn't remembered Miss Gale as well as that. He then saw the girl they called Nell was also present, at the distance usual to her friendly and easier style, and decided to retire no further than within call, if he were called, and he hoped he would be.

And another thing. Young Gale's wits had come back to him, but how would he take this sudden bump, and nothing to ease it? When he saw how the pair greeted each other, he turned away.

He took Nell Tapscott's arm confidentially, and whispered to her that they were not wanted there, not for a spell, and it could be even longer than that, for all he knew, which wasn't much.

FORTY-ONE

It was some weeks after this, when Dr. Pickles, considering at ease his morning news, was shaken by a displacing concussion, sonorous and grave enough for the downfall of the firmament. The surgeon glanced at his window, which nearly fell out. The air of Bewley went on shuddering in lowly response to celestial collapse, even in his room.

The surgeon got up, leisurely, and went to his window, taking his morning paper with him. A near one, that. Another of those handmade meteorites, the rockets; and the closest yet, by the convulsion it set up. He noted, in disbelief, that the trees and chimney pots beyond stood upright as if he alone had been moved by the bursting of the atmosphere. They were undisturbed.

Damnation! This latest novelty of science made havoc of common sense. An instant calamity, and no warning! It sounded just across the road.

Where did it strike? Well, he would never learn that. Nobody would ever know that, except the sufferers. Ignorance officially imposed is more helpful in the lunacy of war than general knowledge. It could always be assumed that what is kept out of the news of war is worse than anything published.

He watched for a minute the traffic on the road. It moved at its usual pace, unaffected. No sign there. Bewley was not hurt, this time. Where the afflicted were was their private concern. He returned to his chair, trailing his paper. He rested his head on the back of it, and pushed his reading glasses above his nose, as if he were weary of circumstance and would repel the sight of it. His loosened hand let his paper fall to the floor, and he didn't know he had dropped it. His mind had gone as listless as his hand.

He was not stricken by languor. He had not made a despairing resolve to give up trying to keep dissolution in fairly good repair. It was only that he had read a minute ago, in unexpected full belief and relief, a column of print in his newspaper. It was a report of battle the day before, in which the outcome was as certain to his understanding as sunrise after a night dark, long, disturbed, confused, and minatory.

His scepticism of all news of the progress of war, as it is studied for public comfort by a censor in a Whitehall back room—his natural disposition, in fact, to doubt reality after it has been strained through the refining minds of experts—such a defect, which he knew was his, did not prevent his full acceptance of what his latest newspaper had been telling him.

There was reason for this. Out of his years of experience in detecting the drift of threat in the vagaries of gunfire, on the desperate field of battle itself, he knew this last report from France had the verity of a stark catalogue of details in the enemy's ruin, while in hurried retreat. This morning there was no doubt about it. None at all. That was why his head rested on the back of his chair.

The day had come. This was it. The day that nobody, once, had dared to think about—here it was. It was today; and stress of mind left him, and it had been stretched and tightened as if time itself must snap. Hitler's flying bombs and falling meteorites had started their improvement on diabolism too late to change destiny; the flames that man had set going were driving backwards in fury to consume him in a shift of wind. The hideous colossus in jackboots that bestrode Europe was giving at the knees, and its sprawl would shake the earth. What came after that was not for him, but the younger men to attend to, God help them.

If but a moment ago he had opened his eyes on simple daylight, released from a prolonged and grisly nightmare, the familiar objects in his room could not have looked more delightfully natural and endearing than they were. The recital of combat he had been pondering over, to which the rocket exploded as the full stop, was freedom from the heavy dread that had shackled everybody since more years ago than could be counted by an elderly man who was sure he could be lazy for a spell.

So his thoughts wandered. They needed a run. They had been bound for a penal period to the day of the week, by fear of the unknown. They had been shut within the hour and could not get out. Now they could please themselves. He had always forbidden them the past. No help was there; but they turned that way, as they will, when released, in those whose vista into the lost years is deep. The time had arrived when the ambiguity in the bygone had lost its menace. The wrong hidden there had issued into full shape in this morning's light. The worst was known. The men who had started the guns once again would die in the wreck of what was to have been their stronghold of power and glory.

Yes. But if only Jupiter—or whoever had taken over his authority—would quash pride with an immediate bolt when a mortal was noticed trying to force others to his will! What waste, to leave it to reason, that uncertain human faculty, and act too late!

Always too late. Too late one blitz night for a child brought to him. There was nothing he could do for her fair head, with the impression of terror still on her face, and he could see it this morning. There was a burial, and she was in it, "child unknown." She was sufficient to condemn them all. He lacked in charity to the men who did that; nothing else was lacking but their necks, the millstones, and the deep sea. Perhaps he felt like that because he was childless.

Now the blow had struck. Thoughts could drift into the past, curious, and no reproach, all solicitude gone for what was in wait, to occasions that would hardly bear looking at, in the hour when it had to be done.

Memory-lighted, isolated far off in the night of the forgotten, was a Cornish street. It was there yet in unfailing distinction, this side the years of our surrender at Munich and the rape of Prague. That was why its holiday glow was not what it ought to have been. The Poles the next to be run over? That meant that we should muster. Children were shoving past with buckets, gay balloons, and cheerful cries. But the black news was there, it came just after early coffee, that Hitler and Stalin were embracing; and they had been bawling hatred over their frontiers for years. The Nazis and Communists were brothers, that holiday time, for a reason agreed between themselves, and kept there, except that they would share loot on the warpath.

What did that mean? How soon should we know? The happy children had no answer. They knew nothing. Their fathers did not know; they only knew that this little Island had not the weight to match both Germany and Russia. And the rumbling of gun-wheels on the roads of Europe could be heard with the sound of doom on the move, even in a Cornish cove. On the beach below, the children were busy building sand castles against an incoming tide.

It was not easy that day in Cornwall for an oldster, who could not forget earth's corruption about Ypres and the Somme, the only solid matter in foul mud a mixture of British and German bones—it was hard for him to believe the Germans were going to extend the hideous, adding more bones. Unless they were mad. Had they gone berserk? So it sounded. Teutonic bellowing against the Poles had the ring of dementia, hate gone loose.

That memory brought Nicholas to sight again; this time, alas, as a shade. It had happened before, when a crisis was too thick for him to see through it, that Nicholas Tregarthen presented himself. No word came beforehand. Trouble could have projected a mentor. There Nicholas was, as a surprise, with his friendly but spectral smile. He came out of nowhere, large and at ease, with his customary expression that life, as usual, was playing the fool. So he showed up in India, one cholera season; and again after the German avalanche swept away our front line in 1918, at St. Quentin. More wounded men were lying about that morning than a miracle-worker could manage; and Nicholas appeared through the smoke and dust, pandemonium with victims being rather more than one man could handle. Most of the cripples were moved beyond the eruptions.

And in a corridor of this hospital, soon after the sharp alarm on a holiday beach in Cornwall, there he was again, and he had never entered the building before. Had I heard? He wanted to know. No, I hadn't. What?

"They've started."

"Started? They've started?"

"Off again. I've just heard from Gale. German bombers are over Poland. I thought you'd better hear. It will make some difference."

Some difference! War was already upon us, while the wounds of the other war were unhealed.

Nicholas knew German as well as he knew anatomy. He had studied in Germany, because of some specialty of his own, and would have it that its philosophers had done more to tangle German thought into fascinating but frightful involutions than the weird sisters worked in the soul of Macbeth. And see what happened to him! It was his idea that it was worth while learning German, if only to read Heine. When you know Heine, he used to say, you can make a fair guess at what may come out of Germany, some day. Then you won't be upset by what is offensive to your civilized eye and nose. After the first war, his derision of the sympathy of some good people for the Germans in their downfall was wicked. Kindly feeling for them amused him. "It's just what they like. It's balm to their self-pity and sentimentality. They ooze it when out of luck. They've been sobbing for years, broken-hearted, over their failure to bring us down. Thor and his hammer, he's theirs, and never forget it. He is their god when they are feeling righteous. Look out, when they start again."

They had started. Nicholas had no mocking little smile that morning. "There is one good thing in it," he remarked, as he turned to go. "Hitler has let loose the Russian bear, and he is nearest to it. That shows what a lunatic he is. Nobody can ever tell what an expressionless bear will do, when loose, not even the bear himself."

After that, during a long and baffled anxiety in a war that America supposed was not war, one Sunday afternoon there was a group in a Surrey garden. A moment came when everybody paused, looked up wondering, looked round, looked at each other. A thudding was in the air, slight but insistent. They had heard that muttering before. The guns!

Then war had reached the Channel coast. No question of it now. France had gone. We were alone, and the enemy was opposite our holiday beaches. All heard the admonition, but nobody spoke. There was something to say, and we could not say it. The trees, the grass, the flowers, the warm sunlight, were in the familiar order of nature, but we left that order a moment ago. We were conjured into an unknown dimension, where the sunlight was wan and cold, and the flowers a pretense.

Moments like that, and they came too often, when the old truths were smiling cheats. Personal survival was nothing much in a world being mutilated and left to putrefy for the honor of madness. Moments suggesting that the bonds which held parent to child, friend to friend, and the planets in their orbits, had all gone. All had fallen apart. We were separate in a blind darkness. What had been absolute was as everlasting as a fly on the ceiling. Looking to the stars, alone at night, the break-up of the Galaxy, the fixed points shooting loose in all directions, would have been witnessed in dismay only because it was further mockery of man's assurance of perennial good.

It wasn't that Germany's bombers and tanks were overwhelming, too swift and heavy for soft humanity to resist. It wasn't that. The person everywhere had come down to the worth of a rat in the gutter. That was what appalled. Morals, he had an idea, are but religion settled into custom and civility. Something different would replace that, and it had the face of an ape. In that obscene confusion the Beatitudes had the appeal of the scratches on a discarded potsherd. Every event was of further treachery and ruin, as on the day when Rotterdam, harmless, unsuspecting, and helpless, was reduced to brickbats and a repository of carrion for blowflies; and even so was in accord with the reek and stench of Europe.

Could it have been, the surgeon considered, that in that act Germany destroyed itself? That a power unknown will not have it so? If one could keep hold of that faith! That there is a purpose destined, and whatever thwarts it must die! It is wise to hold on to it, though there is no arithmetic to prove that the attempt of the liar to corrupt innocence marks his grave. We do know that Hitler was seen to caper, when the message was handed to him that France would surrender. Victory! He danced. Nobody noticed that the immediate happy activity of his legs was very like the spasmodic flexions of limbs dangling from a gallows. Witnessing eyes, those able to surmise reality in the passing minute, might have seen in that brief dance of his, prophetically, where in fact his legs already were. That man rejoiced in a moment of triumph, won by his inflexible will, as he called his self-assertion; but his gallows was up, and he put it up.

It was somewhere about then that he saw a quotation from a Madrid paper, and it expressed grim satisfaction because "the English are corralled." That only told him what he knew, though he did not want to own up to it, not aloud. On all the shores facing us from the Arctic to the Bay of Biscay there the enemy stood, and he completed the circle with his submarines. We were corralled. Darkness extended to the ends of the earth, and no way showed through it. No point of light was anywhere.

No way out by the means and strength we had. Yet one little fact was forgotten. It has no place in the daily rough and tumble over rent and bread. It is never about till dire occasion evokes it from wherever it bides its hour in the mysterious universe. The power of the spirit, quiet and selfless, strives beyond the bounds of reason. High explosives are nothing to it. The bowels can be explained pretty well, and why desires spring up, but not why the mind works when called upon for a purpose above itself, nor what it can do with the impossible. A humble man comes out of his desert dwelling with no more than a conviction of a happier way of life, and the material reign of the magnificoes, palaces, temples, cavalry, spears, and the rest of a dominion of earth, presently shows signs that in the march of the years, pomp and circumstance shine less splendidly than before.

While we were waiting for the sky to fall, a voice was heard in the dark. It was calling to the invisible. It was Churchill. There were listeners, dismayed by the eclipse of the humanities, who heard, and stood up. The sky did not fall. A word in the dark lifted it. A light appeared, and we turned to it. That invocation to the unseen was calm and firm, and perhaps the sky is kept from falling simply by constancy of good will. We knew that voice. We knew it well. Yet it was long since it had been raised with that challenge in the sound of it to the

226

apparition of fate. This Island had spoken. Its call to the universal was the beginning of the end. Today the end was near. Paris was in sunlight again.

The surgeon's head was still resting on the back of his chair, his face composed, as in a last sleep, life's labor past. He did not hear the Matron enter his room. She came in busily, but stopped, alarmed by his surrender to peace. This was not according to rule. Was he unwell? She began to gather up from the floor, still observing him, the untidy scatter of his newspaper sheets. The rustling opened his eyes.

"I thought you must be ill or extremely tired to sleep at this hour."

"Asleep? I was never so wide awake."

"But you didn't hear me come in."

"How could I? I was listening to the cheers in Paris."

"What?"

"It's quite all right. What is there I ought to be doing that I am not doing?"

She remained in doubt. You can't trust a man whose words have several meanings which dodge about, and never to the point. She was further dubious because Dr. Pickles rose in obedience to duty with an alacrity unweighted by the usual delusions of mood and the moment. Why was he so animated?

"I came in to tell you that Stephen and Lucy Gale are here on a visit, and I suppose they'll want to see you."

"Of course they will. This morning was made for it."

The surgeon retained, while alone and waiting for his visitors, the restful fancy that his room was in a gap in space, immune from the clock. A thrush was singing to itself in the shrubbery below. That was all he could hear, a note as usual in brief tranquillity as the silence of the sky.

FORTY-TWO

While Dr. Pickles was still in suspense, time began to move on again. A sportive voice in the corridor without set it going. That certainly was Stephen Gale's note, husky and decisive. Laughter followed. That was Nurse Bridget. So the young fellow was coming along as well as that? He could be fun now, instead of a worry? And yet, more likely than not, he would be unaware that he owed his life to that laughing girl; or was it owing to his late neighbor in the ward, the seaman McLuckie?

Dr. Pickles was amused. In all circumstance, in all nature, just where is the simple thing that will work the trick for sanity, while the trained mind is searching where science says it ought to be, but where rather too often it is not?

No matter. The hospital in general would save the honors. They had much to say to each other. Miss Gale was adding a little to the laughter. This morning's air was light.

He then caught sight of his favored engraving over the mantelpiece, his lucky find in the Charing Cross Road he'd forgotten when, now a secret token of Nicholas Tregarthen: White Stacks, far back among its trees in the past, memory established.

He frowned at it. That wouldn't do. The reminder was, at this moment, inappropriate. And too late to remove it, though to these visitors its innocent suggestion of another day than this could have a damaging thrust. Mental balance is tender.

His door opened, and there the Gales were; and—by the ugly juggling of chance, as though their opening of the door had touched it off—the ascending whine of the air-raid siren began, preliminary to its undulating howl.

Dr. Pickles grimaced in comic dislike of the noise as the two came forward, shaking his head in dismissal of such an old joke about death in the air which everybody had heard before, and didn't want to hear again.

Lucy greeted him. Converse, while that howling continued, would have been too much of a conscious effort; though, by her unwavering glance, she repelled its brutish insistence. Her eyes met his directly, in candor, and, so he imagined, in gratitude. A show of thankfulness always embarrassed him, but he felt no unease while her eyes were on him. Discernment was in them, and good heart. Nicholas once told him that Lucy was limber and shining enough to be one of Diana's nymphs, if cruel to ill-mannered and incautious mortals. No. Not Diana. This girl had a warmth unsuited to the cold moonlight of an esoteric devotion.

The siren ceased its ululations abruptly. The reminiscence of unholy days and nights was brief.

Dr. Pickles turned to seek signs of mastership in his former patient's bearing; and Stephen's composure, while he apologized for bringing the specter's discordant howl into the room with him, was enough. Dr. Pickles wondered what odd coincidence in the man's heritage gave him the height and insouciance of a cavalry officer, which he didn't need, when by all accounts he preferred seclusion with the abstract graces. Perhaps the graces without the aid of masculinity would be barren.

Lucy spoke, and he could see her levity was not of summoned gallantry. "We've been wandering about," she explained. "We were out earlier than you will be able to believe at once. We saw the sun come up over the houses. Yes. We were going up Ludgate Hill. I've never seen anything like it. What kept St. Paul's dome from floating off I don't know. It was on the point of rising into the sky. I've been longing to stand there in that minute. I did this morning."

"Good God."

"Yes. We've been revisiting the glimpses. Have you seen the poor City, since it was burnt out?"

"Now, do I remind you of a ghost? The trouble is, this place keeps me acting as if I were absolutely substantial. Anyhow, I can't pretend to a love for ruins before breakfast."

"Neither can I. Sunrise isn't for ruins. But the ruins came afterwards. It was Stephen's idea."

The doctor noticed that Stephen had sidled away. He

was over by the fireplace. He must have spied that wretched picture, and was brooding over it.

"Stephen thought of it first. He wanted to see whether Paternoster Row was there, and it wasn't. Then he wanted to find out if Milton's Church still exists. I've heard Uncle Nicholas make fun of him over his pilgrimages, over St. Giles—the Cripplegate one—and Bunhill Fields."

"Where? Look here. I don't believe it. You might as well say the Elysian Fields. There's no such place as Bunhill."

"It's on a good map," said Stephen, rejoining them. "You can find it, if you know how to. I didn't, the first time I went. It's Finsbury way. I'd never heard of Finsbury. I'll tell you how to do it. When you've hit on Robinson Crusoe in those fields, and that is easy, you measure twenty-five paces from him northwest, and there is Blake. He is under the footpath, so they say. He's at your feet, if your faith is jolly good."

Dr. Pickles observed the man. The smile on his lean visage was constant, if ironically appraising. "Did your faith keep faith, that day?"

"Of course. Blake is everywhere, so he must be there. We didn't get as far as the fields at Bunhill today."

"I wasn't going to try," said Lucy. "We gave up by Aldersgate Street. I wasn't tired, not a bit, but I soon had enough of those dreary empty gaps that haven't been seen in London since that other great fire. Stephen pretended he knew his way about, but I could see he was lost, and didn't want to say so."

"There is nothing to go by, except mistakes," Stephen admitted. "No landmarks. All gone. Wiped out. On one side of Aldersgate Street is open air as far as you can see outlines of things you don't recognize. It's as dead as the moon. St. Giles' tower is there, though, all alone, standing up in the middle of extinction. How could I be sure of it from where we were on a splintered curbstone? But we found old Milton afterwards. He's still there. I don't care what anybody says. We found him, face downwards in thistles and willow herb. He is all right, except for his nose, which used to be a good one. They can't get rid of him. He belongs to us. Another thing is, do you know the Bread Street plane tree is in full leaf this summer? Well, it is. It is alive, and you'd wonder why."

Heritage and tradition, mused the doctor. These two preserved a vitality in the land as natural as its flints, sure to show itself when the season comes round, like the roots in the desert, true to type. We get as much of immortality as we earn.

"You've brought me news I like," Dr. Pickles told them. "The sun must have seen you were out of doors, and wanted to give support. It's time you had some coffee. I'll ring . . ."

"No," said Lucy. "Thank you, but we had breakfast at a street canteen. A group of firemen invited us. They were soaking wet, and their faces smeared with charcoal, and it was fun. We must be on our way again soon. We're taking Stephen's friend the sailor to his ship. He sails this afternoon."

232

"Off again, is he? I wish I were coming with you. I've some right to see that man delivered intact to his native deck, but you do it for me. Let me know that he is parted from the shore, and soon. I'll say that McLuckie gives me more confidence than I ever seem to have given him."

"Yes. Stephen has been telling me about him. He looks at me, I must say, as if I were at a distance, and he wasn't sure how far off."

"What, even you? Well, your brother must know that he was the only one here to get anything from McLuckie except flippancy. I've watched them with their heads together in conspiracy. If that fellow feels he is safe with St. Peter at the gate, then he will keep the old boy all attention while the queue for admission piles up. His name, which I don't believe, is against it, but he seems to me to be the Cockney of the legend, as old as sin, and so used to the upsetting of his applecart that he only looks wryly at the wreck, and fills his pipe. But he is always on his guard, of course, because he knows his amiable nature may let in somebody to his undoing."

"I'd go anywhere with him," muttered Stephen.

"Not today," said Lucy, "not yet."

The surgeon went with them to the hospital gates. "I don't like the thought of this ride through the dock country," he was saying to Lucy. "I've been through it. You be ready for it, please. East London isn't the same as the dreary gaps in the City. For me, it was a sad reminder of Flanders. You will see a desolation of homes, whole parishes, and wide. Wide beyond dreariness.

233

What happened there won't bear thinking about, so don't you do it. . . . Why, there McLuckie is. And he didn't come to see me."

"He said he preferred to wait."

"I see. So he did. Of course he did. Now we see why. That is your maid with him, isn't it? He is not strictly on his guard with her, is he?"

Lucy, whose regard of the pair before her had been strict, now smiled. Nellie certainly had won the sailor's confidence, to say the least of it. They might have known each other since childhood.

"He has the eye," commented Dr. Pickles, "and she has the shape in full. You had better call it a good omen for your prospect of broken homes. The past, the best of it, most likely is quite safe, though it doesn't look like it—there's the people who will bring it up to date and keep it going." He looked about. "What has become of your brother?"

"He went to speak to the Matron, and then Miss Bridget came along."

"And after all," continued Dr. Pickles, "those ruins, that rubbish. Bad as it is, you'll come to a ship in the middle of it, with steam up. You'll come to that. She'll be humming to herself, with a white wisp at her funnel. I've seen it. Yes, I know . . . Here, I must speak to that man at the gate before he goes. What a thing to be young, and outward bound!"

FORTY-THREE

A morning came to Bewley when nothing but wisps of cirrus were aloft in the sky. The sky above us was luminous, simple, ample, and satisfying, and could be disregarded. The war was over. Evil, promoted to the eternal vault by human ingenuity, to darken it, had gone, so anxious eyes were lowered from the everlasting. As in the beginning, the heavens were only the source of light and bounty.

It was also April. With the end of gunfire and night fears had come the season on earth for life's awakening; and the conventional unfolding of cherry, laburnum, and lilac made morning as phenomenal as if this had happened in England for the first time. To the children it was for the first time, and to others it was as though the lambency of the uprising had been kept in abeyance till it would accord, as it did that morning, with whoever had eyes free to look and wonder.

With this revival, the approach to White Stacks was inviting with color and fragrance; for a Lady Gale, in days gone by, had shown refinement in the choice of species and varieties for planting. The approach was without let or hindrance. Anybody could go in. Its gates

235

were better than open; they were absent. Even their tim-
ber supports had gone, as fuel thereabouts had been
scarce for years. There were raw breaks in the enclosing
walls. The entrance to a personal and cherished ground,
with a name conspicuous on maps that are out of date,
and preserved here and there in the annals of England,
had the suggestion of a casual track leading to a nameless quarter abandoned as unprofitable nobody knew
when.

Two men sauntered within. They have not appeared
elsewhere in this record, and as newcomers they are too
late to play a part in it. Whatever could have drawn
them into the place that morning must be left to the
chance that its promise for progress will become known
to others later on, truth for history that is to be written.
It did not seem that they were aware of White Stacks.
It must have been new to them. Nor did they pause to
admire and question the burgeoning of shrubs that are
not commonly seen.

They surveyed broadly that large vacancy amid a
crowding suburb. "Plenty of room here," said one to the
other, "and it won't last like this. Doesn't it strike you
as just what is wanted?"

"That's what I thought."

"Who's the owner? The first thing to do is to find him
before things settle down. It doesn't look as if anybody
was keen about it."

They sauntered on. They came to the area, shaggy
with weeds, where a house once stood. Two other visitors were there, silently gazing at it. The two men, in a

perfunctory glance, were reassured. Those two young people could not be rivals. They had not that manner. They were there only to see what was there.

"Look at that," said one man to the other. "Not much leveling wanted, is there? And a chalk foundation. It's a bed ready made."

The two young people moved away slowly, as if aware this was private ground, and they might be unwelcome but that they had no ill intent.

"What was it that fellow said?" asked Stephen, when they were out of hearing.

"I wasn't listening," said Lucy. "I did hear him say something about development, that's all."

A puzzling word. There was a dry laugh between them.

"It is so tidy now," she explained to Stephen, "but it was terrible, when I first saw it. It was a great heap. Nothing was on it we knew, only a little showing, and, of all we had, Mother's piano. It was upside down. I haven't been here since, and I never thought you'd want to come."

"What? You saw that, dead? You saw that? You tell me you saw that, and were alone?"

"One day."

Stephen stopped, and surveyed his sister. "What a girl you are. My stars, you beat me."

"You couldn't come with me, you know, and it had to be done."

He rested a hand on her shoulder, and looked away.

"We still have its music," he said. "They can't kill that."

"Do you hear it?" asked Lucy. "I can hear it. I hear it better than ever, when alone. Sometimes I wish I couldn't hear it so well, but it will come back."

"It is very important," said Stephen.

They strolled deeper into the seclusion. They tried to distinguish the remembered best things of a garden—the roses, the herbs—but the wild had been too much for the civility of the past.

"This," said Stephen, "is the secret path Nick used going to the lake, when he was getting away from us, and didn't want to be seen."

"I know," said Lucy. "I used to see him escaping. From my bedroom window it was no secret. I hated him for it, then."

"Not now?"

"All gone. He knew more than I did, and some of it he knew better. And I think he felt it, too. Yes, I believe he felt it. . . . Hate is silly."

"Just here," said Stephen, within the alcove of the yews, "is where I had a long talk with him, not long before it happened."

There was a disturbance on the surface of the water before them, and the glistening of a large body, partly revealed.

Stephen cried out, "And there's the very same carp, I do believe. He was here that morning, and he's still about. . . . Dear God, and the rest all gone. What's to be made of that?"

"Don't try to make anything of it. I won't, any more. Once there was another garden, worse for the man who was in it than this is for us. Yet it was not the end. It was the beginning."

Stephen was silent.

He asked presently, "What do you believe? Would you call this a beginning? It doesn't look like a beginning, does it?"

"I suppose it never does. But it must be, it must be. It is, for us. I don't know what I believe. It changes. Sometimes I'm quite sure, and the next day I'm nearly all dark again. But I'm always quite sure of one thing. It's what we've heard called the Holy Ghost. That comes. I can't tell you any more. It keeps me quiet."

ABOUT THE AUTHOR

HENRY MAJOR TOMLINSON was born in 1873 and has had a long and distinguished career as a journalist and author. He has had a score of travel books, essays and novels published, which have won him esteem as a master of prose. His first book, *The Sea and the Jungle* (1912), tells of a voyage aboard a tramp steamer and of a trek through two thousand miles of Brazilian jungle. It was immediately acclaimed, and is today recognized as a classic of travel literature. It has appeared in the Modern Library series and is now available as a Modern Library Paperback. Among Tomlinson's other best-known works are *Tidemarks, All Our Yesterdays* and *Gallions Reach*. THE TRUMPET SHALL SOUND, his first novel in many years, has been long awaited by H. M. Tomlinson's legion of admirers.